Chapter 1

I kept shouting to her, but Aunt Lucy didn't seem to hear. I followed her along one corridor after another, but no matter how hard I tried, I couldn't catch up with her.

"Aunt Lucy! Wait! Aunt Lucy, wait for me!"

Where were we, anyway? What was this building? I didn't recognise it. There were no doors—just corridor after corridor. Eventually, she reached a staircase.

I shouted again, "Aunt Lucy! It's Jill! Wait for me!"

I made my way slowly down the stairs, and as I neared the bottom, I could see Aunt Lucy in the distance. She was standing in front of a door. I knew instinctively that there was danger behind that door—something evil.

"Aunt Lucy! Don't open that door!"

At long last, she turned around to face me. "It's okay, Jill. There's nothing to worry about."

"No! Aunt Lucy, it's dangerous! Don't open that door!"

She turned the handle.

I sat up in bed—in a cold sweat.

Jack was nowhere to be seen, but then I remembered he'd told me the night before that he had an early start. I felt exhausted from the dream. It was horrible! Thank goodness I'd woken up.

Even after I'd showered, dressed, and eaten breakfast, I couldn't shake the images of that dream. I'd had nightmares before, but there was something about this one that had really disturbed me. Could it have been some sort of subconscious message? Maybe Aunt Lucy was ill or in trouble.

I magicked myself over to her house, but when I

knocked on the door, there was no reply. Now I was starting to get worried. Aunt Lucy was always an early riser; she should have been up by now. I knocked again. Still no reply. Maybe I'd been right; maybe the dream had been a sign.

As always, her front door was unlocked, so I let myself in. Once inside, I heard raised voices. Aunt Lucy and Lester were arguing; they always seemed to be arguing these days. I hated turning up like this in the middle of an argument, but I still wanted to make sure everything was okay, so I knocked on the kitchen door.

"It's only me."

"Come in, Jill. You don't have to knock."

Lester was sitting at the kitchen table. He was dressed, but Aunt Lucy was still in her dressing gown.

"I'm sorry to call on you unannounced."

"You don't have to apologise for coming to see us, Jill. You're welcome anytime. I was just going to make some toast. Would you like some?"

"No, thanks. I've had breakfast. I just wanted to check that you were okay."

"Why wouldn't I be? Is there something the matter?"

"Nothing, really. I just had a horrible dream. You and I were in a strange building that I'd never seen before. I was following you down lots of corridors. I was trying to catch up with you, but I couldn't. I called to you, but you didn't hear me—then we went down some stairs. You were about to open a door, and I could sense there was something dangerous or evil behind it. I told you not to open it, but you did it anyway."

"And was there? Something evil, I mean?"

"I don't know. That's when I woke up."

"I have horrible nightmares too sometimes. I wouldn't worry about it. Is Jack okay?"

"Yeah, Jack's fine. He'd gone to work before I even woke up. Anyway, I suppose I ought to get back."

"Don't go yet. Sit down and have a cup of tea."

"I really should go."

"I've got custard creams."

"Mmm – go on then."

Aunt Lucy brought out the Tupperware box filled with my favourite biscuits. What better way to start the day than a cup of tea and custard creams?

"You're looking very smart, Lester," I said.

"I've started my new job."

"Of course. How's it going?"

"Don't ask," Aunt Lucy said.

"Is there a problem?" I could sense that Lester was annoyed.

"If you must know, Jill. Your aunt is jealous."

"I am not jealous," Aunt Lucy snapped.

"What else would you call it?"

"I am *not* jealous. Why would I be jealous of *that* person?"

"That person?" I'd just finished my second custard cream, and was wondering whether I should have another.

"Your aunt is referring to my 'buddy'."

"Is that what you call her?" Aunt Lucy replaced the lid on the Tupperware box. Drat!

"As I was saying," Lester continued. "All new Grim Reaper trainees are assigned to a more experienced operative who they work with on a kind of buddy system."

"More experienced, my backside." Aunt Lucy was determined to have her say. "What can she possibly know about anything?"

"See? This is what I mean," Lester said. "Lucy is annoyed because my 'buddy' is a young woman."

"Woman?" Aunt Lucy interrupted. "She's barely out of school!"

"She's twenty-one!"

Aunt Lucy joined us at the table. "What can she possibly know about anything?"

"Her parents are Grim Reapers, and she's been working as one since she was eighteen. She's fully qualified, and she's my buddy."

"She's your buddy, alright. Too buddy buddy for my liking."

"Enough, Lucy!" Lester thumped the table. "Monica is a very good tutor, and I'm lucky to have her."

"Says you."

There was a knock at the door.

"That'll be her." Lester was about to stand up, but Aunt Lucy beat him to it, and hurried to the front door.

"Come in. He's in the kitchen."

Aunt Lucy showed the young woman in. Monica was a stunner with beautiful, long, curly brown hair, a complexion to die for, and a great figure. She had the most gorgeous smile.

"Hiya, Lessie!"

Lessie?

"Morning, Monica." Lester beamed.

"Are you ready for your next day's training?"

"Ready and willing!" Lester stood up, grabbed his bag, and followed her. "Bye, Jill. Bye, Lucy." He tried to give

Aunt Lucy a kiss, but she turned her face to one side, so he only brushed her cheek.

"See ya, everybody," Monica said, and the two of them disappeared out of the door.

"Do you see what I mean, Jill?" Aunt Lucy was still seething.

"She seems pleasant enough."

"Pleasant? Don't give me 'pleasant.' I don't trust her."

"How's his training going, anyway?"

"All right, or so he says. I still don't know why he took this job. I've been trying to persuade him to look for something else, but unbelievably he seems to be enjoying it. Can you imagine?" She shuddered.

"Apart from the whole Monica thing, are you okay, Aunt Lucy?"

"I'm fine. I shouldn't let it get to me. Anyway, let's forget about Lester and his *buddy*. I've got something to show you."

"Anything exciting?"

"I think so." She glanced through the window. "After all the problems I've had with gardeners recently, I've decided to look after the garden myself. The only problem is that I find mowing the lawn hard work. But when I went into Candlefield the other day, you'll never guess what I found."

I was getting bad vibes about this already.

"An enchanted mower!" She beamed.

"Enchanted? What does that mean, exactly?"

"Sorry. I should have explained. The mower has a mind of its own. Well, sort of. I don't fully understand it myself."

"I didn't realise it was possible to enchant things."

"Only the most powerful level six witches are able to cast the 'enchantment' spell. I'm surprised that you didn't come across it in Magna Mondale's book."

"Come to think of it, I do remember seeing a section on enchantment, but at the time I didn't think it was something I'd ever have a use for."

"Come outside, and I'll give you a demonstration."

Aunt Lucy led the way out to the garden. I stayed just outside the back door while she walked over to the shed, and fetched the lawnmower. On the face of it, it looked just like every other lawnmower I'd ever seen.

"What do you think?" Aunt Lucy was glowing with pride.

"It's, err—it's very nice. It doesn't look particularly enchanted, though?"

"Just watch." Aunt Lucy addressed the lawnmower. "Matilda!"

"Matilda?"

"All enchanted objects are given a name, so they know when you're speaking to them."

"Of course."

"Matilda, cut the lawn!"

Suddenly, the lawnmower sprang to life. It edged its way slowly to one side of the lawn, but then took off apace. It sped to the other side, spun around so quickly that it almost tipped over, and then shot back. It repeated this time after time.

"Are you sure we're safe here, Aunt Lucy?" The lawnmower had started to head towards us.

"Perfectly safe. Matilda knows where the edge of the lawn is."

The lawnmower was moving so quickly that I was

convinced it was going to leave the grass, and crash into us. I closed my eyes, but then heard it skid around, and start back in the opposite direction.

"It's good, isn't it?" Aunt Lucy said. "Just look how quickly it can get the job done."

"It's certainly quick, but it does seem awfully dangerous."

"Not at all. Matilda is as safe as houses."

***

After leaving Aunt Lucy's, I made my way over to Cuppy C. Laura and Flora were behind the counter. When they saw me, they smiled. There was something about that pair I didn't trust, but I couldn't quite put my finger on it. I was just about to ask them where the twins were when I heard raised voices coming from over in the corner. Amber and Pearl were obviously arguing about something. Nothing new there.

"Hi, you two."

"Hiya, Jill," Amber said.

"Morning, Jill," Pearl said.

"Is it okay if I join you?"

"Yeah, of course. Take a seat."

They were both still looking daggers at one another.

"What's the matter with you two? What are you arguing about this time?"

"Amber doesn't know how to add up," Pearl said.

"Yes, I do. I checked it, double checked it, and triple checked it. The figures are right."

"They can't possibly be right!"

"What figures are you talking about?" I asked.

"Yesterday's takings," Pearl said. "Amber must have made a mistake when she cashed up."

"I did not make a mistake! You can go and check for yourself; the money's still in the safe!"

"I don't need to check it. We can't possibly have taken that amount of money yesterday."

"Are the takings down?" If they were, I knew who my prime suspects would be: The two ice maidens.

"No, they're not down," Pearl said. "They're up!"

Colour me confused. "Surely that's good, isn't it?"

"Yes and no. Having more money is good, but we can't possibly have earned this amount from what was sold yesterday. It doesn't make any sense. Unless Amber miscounted."

"I did not miscount." Amber was losing patience with her sister. "When I counted it last night, I knew the figures seemed wrong. That's why I checked it, and checked it again. I still got the same amount."

"Impossible!"

"Possible!"

It was time to change the subject. "How did the housewarming parties go? Was a good time had by all?"

The way the twins were glaring at me suggested that the answer to that question probably wasn't 'yes.'

"It was a total disaster," Pearl said.

"Oh? Why?"

I hadn't been able to attend the house warming-athon because I'd come down with a bad tummy.

What? You would have made an excuse too if you'd been in my shoes. One housewarming is bad enough, but two in one day? I don't think so.

"The bus turned up at the wrong house because Amber

gave them incorrect instructions." Pearl rolled her eyes.

"No, I didn't," Amber spat back. "You were the one who told them where to go."

"No I didn't. That was your job!"

"So, what happened exactly?" I said.

Amber sighed. "The bus was meant to turn up at my house at four-thirty to take all the guests and me over to Pearl's. But it went to the wrong house—it went to Pearl's."

"What happened then?"

"It had to turn around, and come over to my place. We lost three-quarters of an hour right there."

"Surely, that wasn't the end of the world?"

"It wouldn't have been if the bus hadn't broken down on its way from my house to Pearl's. It took another hour to get that sorted, so by the time we got there, we were almost two hours late. All the guests were totally fed up by then. You can imagine what kind of party we had after that. And then to top it all, the bus driver forgot to load the presents, so Pearl's gifts are still at my house."

"Oh dear. But, apart from that, did everything go okay?"

They glared at me again.

Chapter 2

My phone rang. It was Kathy.

"Hi, Jill. How are you?"

"Okay, thanks. You sound very bright."

She was way too bubbly for that time in the morning. Normally, it was almost impossible to get two words out of her so early in the day.

"I have big news."

"Something good, by the sound of it."

"You must promise not to say a word to anyone."

"Okay."

"I mean it, Jill. Not to Jack. Or Mrs V. And definitely not to your grandmother."

"Okay. I promise."

"You know Lucinda Gray, don't you?"

"The name doesn't ring a bell."

"She's the news anchor on Wool TV."

"Oh, *that* Lucinda Gray. No, still never heard of her."

"She's a minor celebrity in wool circles."

"I'm going to have to take your word for that."

"There's a rumour going around that she's landed herself a new job at another TV station. If she leaves, that'll mean there's a vacancy on the news desk."

"Do you think you might get the job?"

"Why not? I'm already presenting the weekly magazine show on Wool TV. It's the logical next step."

"But you've only been there five minutes."

"Yes, but you've seen all the rave reviews I've been getting, haven't you?"

"I can't say I have."

"I've got four and five star reviews from all the yarn

magazines."

"Are there many of those? Yarn magazines?"

"Are you kidding? There are dozens of them. The next time you go into the supermarket, just take a look at the magazine racks. They all love my show. I've started a scrapbook, and pasted all the reviews into it. I can let you borrow it sometime if you'd like?"

"Sure." It sounded like the perfect cure for insomnia.

"Anyway, who else are they going to give the job to? The only other option would be to bring in someone from outside. I don't want to count my chickens though because she might not even be leaving, but fingers crossed, eh?"

"Yeah. Fingers crossed."

"I'd better go. Pete's calling me. See you."

"Bye."

Wow! Kathy, news anchor at Wool TV? How would I cope if my sister became such an 'A' list celebrity?

***

"This is for you." The man at the toll booth held up the latest copy of Mr Ivers' newsletter.

"Is it really that time again, already?"

"Yeah. Mr Ivers insisted I get it to you as soon as possible. He knew you'd be counting the days until the next issue. He said you'd particularly like the article on page three."

"Right. Thanks."

"That will be three pounds ninety-five." The man held out his hand. "Plus forty pence for the toll."

"I don't suppose you'd like to keep the newsletter for

yourself, would you?"

"I've already read it."

"You've read my newsletter?"

"The first couple of pages, but then I fell asleep."

I handed him the money, and threw the newsletter onto the back seat.

When I walked into the office, I was taken aback by the sight that greeted me.

"Mrs V?" She was head down on the desk. It looked like she'd collapsed. "Are you all right?"

Mrs V was prone to the odd funny turn.

I touched her shoulder, and she jumped up. What a relief! It was only when she sat up that I realised she was wearing a sweatband around her head, and was dressed in a lime green leotard.

"Jill, you scared me to death. I must have nodded off."

"Are you feeling all right? I thought you were poorly."

"No, dear. I'm not poorly—just exhausted."

"Why are you wearing the leotard?"

"Didn't you know? I-Sweat is now open. One of those young men came by and left three one-month free trial passes. One for me, one for Jules, and one for you. I put yours on your desk."

"You've just been around there, I take it?"

"Yes. I need to get into shape, ready for Armi's dinner and dance at the Cuckoo Clock Appreciation Society. Not long to go now."

"You haven't overdone it, have you?"

"Possibly. I don't really understand how those treadmill things work."

"What happened?"

"A kind young man showed me how to switch it on, but he didn't really explain how I was meant to stop it."

"Couldn't you have just called him over?"

"It was difficult, because I was facing the window, and all the instructors were behind me. I daren't look around in case I lost my balance and fell off."

"What did you do?"

"I had to keep running until one of the instructors walked by. When one eventually did, he said I should just press the big red button."

"How long had you been on it?"

"I'm not sure, dear. I think it must have been about twenty-five minutes."

"You're supposed to gradually build up the time you spend on the equipment. You could have done yourself a mischief."

"I know, dear. I'm suffering for it now. My knees will never be the same again. And as for my big toe, would you like to see it?"

"No. Thanks all the same."

"Don't forget, Jill. Your free pass is on your desk."

"Okay. I take it you'll be getting changed?"

"Yes. As soon as I've caught my breath, I'll limp down to the loo, and get changed into something more appropriate. Besides, I'll need to squeeze the sweat out of this leotard."

"Lovely."

"Would you like a cup of tea, Jill?"

"No, I think I'll give it a miss. Thanks."

When I walked through to my office, Winky was sitting cross-legged on the sofa. I couldn't see his face because it was buried in a glossy magazine. I leaned a little closer so

I could see what he was reading.

"FQ? What's that?"

Winky lowered the magazine. "Haven't you heard of it? It's Feline Quality."

"It looks a bit up-market for you."

"You could be right, but Bella insisted that I read it. She's taken out a subscription for me. She reckons I'm a bit too rough around the edges."

"What does she expect you to do about it?"

"Apparently, I have to up my game if I want to carry on going out with her. Bella says she can't be seen with someone who's uncouth. Uncouth, me?" He wiped his nose with his paw. "I'm not uncouth, am I?"

"Not at all. Surely, she should love you for who you are?"

"Try telling her that." He shrugged. "If I don't do what she asks, then I think she's going to dump me. She's even arranged for me to take elocution lessons."

I laughed. "Are you serious?"

"Yeah, somebody's coming around here later."

"Oh, boy. Can I watch?"

"No. It'll be embarrassing enough as it is. Who cares if it's raining in Spain? It's all nonsense. And besides, there's nothing wrong with the way I speak. I speak as proper as the next person."

When my first appointment of the day arrived, I was relieved to see that Mrs V had changed out of the sweat-soaked leotard.

"There's a lady here to see you, Jill," Mrs V said. "It's a Mrs Travers. She's just picking out some socks."

"Right, okay. Send her through as soon as she's made

her selection."

A few minutes later, Mrs Travers came through to my office. She was carrying a pair of red and green striped socks, and had a puzzled look on her face.

"Your receptionist just gave me some socks?"

"She does that. Socks or scarves, usually."

"These are very nice. I thought I could hang them up at Christmas."

"Good idea. Do have a seat, Mrs Travers."

"Call me Sarah, please. Mrs Travers makes me sound like my mother."

Sarah Travers was in her late thirties. An attractive woman, who didn't have a particularly good dress sense. The purple blouse simply did not work with the green skirt. Not that I was judging.

"You mentioned something about your husband when you rang?"

"Jerry, yes. I never thought I'd employ a private investigator, but I feel like this has gone on long enough. I need some answers, even if I don't like what you find."

"Do I take it that you think he might be cheating on you?"

"Possibly. I don't know. None of it makes any sense. Do you deal with a lot of infidelity cases?"

"Unfortunately, yes. What is it that gives you cause for concern?"

"About once a month, Jerry tells me that he's going to play squash, but I know he's lying."

"How so?"

"I happened to bump into a woman I know, who works at the leisure club, and she told me that they closed down the squash court some months ago."

"Have you asked him about it?"

"I know I should have, but I didn't know how to broach the subject."

"And you say he does this just once a month?"

"Yes. That's the bit that I don't understand. Surely, if he was having an affair, he'd want to see whoever it was, more than just once a month, wouldn't he?"

"I would have thought so. Usually in the cases I see, it can be several times a week."

"That's what I thought."

"Is it possible that it's not an affair? Could he be doing something else?"

"I suppose so, but I can't think what."

"When did this start?"

"It's always been the same. He's always gone to play squash once a month, but never more than that. When we first got together, I thought it was very strange that he didn't want to play more often."

"Could he be going to a different club?"

"The only other squash club in Washbridge is on the other side of town. And anyway, I asked him if he still went to the Lilac Leisure Club, and he said he did. I don't know what to think. It's got to the point now where I just need to know what's going on. Even if it's bad news, I'd rather know, which is why I came to see you. Do you think you can help?"

"I'll certainly try. Is there a particular date each month that he goes?"

"No, but there's always about a month in between."

"How much notice does he normally give you?"

"He usually tells me on the day. The other thing I should have mentioned is that on those nights, he's always very late back. When I asked why, he said that they go for drinks afterwards, and that it usually stretches out until the early hours of the morning."

Her mention of the late nights added credence to her suspicions that her husband might be cheating on her.

"I think the only way we can do this, Sarah, is if you give me a call the next time he tells you he's going to play squash. I'll tail him, find out where he goes and what he gets up to, and report back. How does that sound?"

"That's great, thanks."

"I'll need a photograph of him."

"Of course. If you give me your email address, I can send you one over."

"Great. It's agreed then. The next time your husband announces that he's going out to play squash, give me a call straightaway, and I'll follow him, and let you know exactly what's going on."

"Thanks very much, Jill."

Chapter 3

Mrs V popped her head around my door.

"Sorry, Jill. I had a phone call while you were talking to Mrs Travers. It's your grandmother. She'd like you to pop down there to see her."

My heart sank. "Did she say what it was about?"

"No. I did ask, but she said it was none of my business, and that you had to get down there as quickly as possible. I asked if she could come up here, but she said that you've got younger legs than she has, so you can do the walking."

"Charming. I suppose I'd better go or I'll be in trouble."

When I stepped out of the office, I noticed a bus go past with Ever a Wool Moment advertising on the side. It was back to normal. I'd seen a few other buses and taxis over the previous few days, and they'd all had the correct wording on them. Whatever Grandma had said or done to Ma Chivers, it had obviously had the desired effect.

As I was walking down the high street, I spotted a man-sized fish on the pavement ahead of me. Next to it was a man-sized crab. And behind those two, was what appeared to be a man-sized seahorse. All three of them were handing out flyers. As I got closer, the seahorse handed one to me.

"There you go." The voice came from inside the seahorse costume.

It was obviously a promotion for the new shop that had opened across the road from Ever. 'She Sells' belonged to my old friend, and ex-tax inspector, Betty Longbottom.

At that precise moment, Grandma came charging out of Ever.

"Hey, you, fishface! And you, crab! And you, horse or whatever you're meant to be—get away from my shop. You're blocking my window. Get back to your own side of the street, or I shall be forced to do something that you'll regret."

The seahorse, crab, and fish weren't in any mood to argue with Grandma, so as soon as there was a break in the traffic, they hobbled across the road.

"You wanted to see me, Grandma?"

"Took you long enough, didn't it? I was three years younger when I left the message."

"I think you may be exaggerating a little."

"Let's go through to the back."

Kathy was behind the counter, but I didn't get a chance to speak to her because she was busy with customers. Grandma led the way into her office.

"What's wrong with that sister of yours?" she said.

"What do you mean?"

"She seems to have her head in the clouds. Twice yesterday, someone complained that they were given the wrong change. Does she have problems at home?"

"Not that I'm aware of."

"I suspect it's that other job of hers. I know I gave her permission to do the Wool TV thing, but it was on the strict understanding that it wouldn't affect her work here. I'm beginning to regret my decision. I'm just too giving, that's my problem."

How I didn't laugh, I will never know.

"I'm sure it's nothing, Grandma. Maybe she didn't sleep very well."

"I don't sleep well either. I'm too busy worrying that my staff might give away all of my hard-earned money."

"Is that why you wanted to see me? To ask about Kathy?"

"Of course not, I just thought I'd mention that while you're here. I have much more important things to discuss with you. Sit down."

I took a seat, as instructed.

"You do realise what will be happening soon, don't you?"

"Your birthday?"

"It's the Levels Competition!"

"Of course."

"Have you started your practice regime?"

"What practice regime?"

"I take it that's a 'No'."

"To be honest, I didn't plan on practising beforehand. I thought I'd just turn up on the day, and see how it went."

She grabbed a handful of her hair in each hand. "You thought you'd turn up on the day and see how it went?"

I thought for a moment she was going to explode.

"Err—yeah."

"I don't think so. Look, young lady, it's not so very long ago since you were given the opportunity of a lifetime: to move to level seven. But for reasons known only to you and that teeny little brain of yours, you turned the offer down. So, it's essential that you at least progress to level six in the quickest possible time. And the best way to do that is to win the Levels Competition outright. Got it?"

"I'll give it my best shot."

"You'd better give it more than that. How do you think I'm going to look if my granddaughter, who is *supposedly* the most powerful witch in Candlefield, can't win the Levels Competition?"

"I get the message. I'll definitely put some practice in."

"A *lot* of practice."

"Okay, I'll put a lot of practice in."

"Maybe I should act as your trainer."

"No need for that. I'm disciplined enough to do my own training."

She gave me a doubtful look. "You better had."

As I walked back to my office, I thought about the Levels Competition. When I'd last competed in it, I'd been a lowly level two witch, and the expectations on me had been non-existent. I'd actually done far better than I could ever have hoped. I deliberately hadn't entered last year's competition because I was still trying to come to terms with everything that had happened to me, but I couldn't avoid it again this year. The expectations on me this time would be way higher. People said that I was the most powerful witch in Candlefield, and that might or might not be true, but it put an awful lot of pressure on me. Anything other than my winning the Levels Competition would be seen as a failure. I wasn't looking forward to it, and I certainly hadn't been planning to put in any practice, but now Grandma had a bee in her bonnet, I might have to.

As I hurried upstairs to the office, I bumped into Brent, one of the two I- Sweat guys.

"Hi, Jill, how's it going?"

"All right." I tried to catch my breath after running up the stairs.

"You don't look very fit. You need to introduce a fitness regime into your life. Did Mrs V give you the one-month free trial pass that I left for you?"

"Yes, she did mention something about it."

"So, when are you going to have your first session?"

"I don't think it's for me."

"Come on, Jill, you want to get fit, don't you?"

"I suppose so."

"Well then, make sure you book your first session soon. Mrs V was really going for it this morning. I've never seen anyone spend so much time on the treadmill."

While I was talking to Brent, I could hear music coming from behind me. When he finally went on his way, and I opened the door to my offices, I discovered the source of that music. Mrs V and Armi were dancing what to the untrained eye looked like the foxtrot. They'd pushed back the furniture to clear a space in the centre of the outer office, and seemed totally oblivious to my presence.

I coughed. "Ahem! Excuse me?" I finally caught their attention, and they stopped dancing.

"Jill? Sorry, I didn't see you there." Mrs V's knee had apparently recovered from the earlier treadmill trauma.

Armi was all smiles.

"Hi, Armi. How are things at Armitage, Armitage, Armitage and Poole?"

"Pretty much the same."

"What about Gordon?"

"He's definitely the same—no better. Fortunately, I don't have much to do with him these days. I think he's given up on me, which is definitely a good thing."

"You're dancing?" I had a talent for stating the obvious.

"We have to practise, Jill," Mrs V said. "The Cuckoo Clock Appreciation Society dinner and dance is looming. We need to grab every opportunity. I hope you don't mind us practising here."

"I suppose not, just as long as I have no appointments

booked."

Mrs V took hold of Armi's hand and they continued to foxtrot around the room. I managed to squeeze past them, and made my way into my office. As soon as I stepped inside, Winky came running up to me.

"What's that dreadful noise out there?"

"Mrs V and Armi are practising ballroom dancing."

"That music is terrible."

"It's not that bad."

"Can't you get them to stop?"

"They need to practise. They've got a dinner and dance coming up. Anyway, they'll be done soon because Armi will have to get back to work."

Winky sighed, put on his ear defenders, and retreated underneath the sofa.

An hour or so later, I heard sounds of furniture being scraped across the floor as Mrs V and Armi moved everything back. Then I heard Armi shout goodbye. Not long after that, Mrs V popped her head around the office door again.

"There's someone to see you, Jill. It's that accountant man."

"Luther? I wasn't expecting him today."

"No, not *that* accountant man. The other one; the one you had before you changed to Mr Stone."

"Robert Roberts? I suppose you'd better show him in."

The last time I'd seen Robert Roberts, he'd been dressed all hipster style, and had informed me that he was giving up his accountancy practice to become a food critic. But the man in front of me today was dressed in a plain suit, white shirt, grey tie, and was once again the archetypal accountant.

"Hello, Miss Gooder."

"Hello, Mr Roberts. What brings you here?"

"You may recall that the last time I paid you a visit, I told you that I'd decided to quit the world of accountancy?"

"Yes. You said you were going to become a food critic."

"I'm not really sure what came over me back then. I can only put it down to a knock on the head. I'd been clearing out the garage when I banged my head on the door. Anyway, I'm pleased to say that I have now regained my senses, and have reinstated the accountancy business. Unfortunately, while in my delusional state, I managed to fire all of my clients."

"I can see how that might be a problem."

"What I'm doing now is inviting them to re-join my practice. That's why I'm here today. I wonder if you'd like to carry on where we left off, so to speak?"

"I'm sorry, Mr Roberts, but I've moved my business to Luther Stone."

"Ah, yes, Mr Stone. I'm aware of him."

"He's doing a very good job for me. I couldn't simply drop him."

"What if I was to offer to provide the same service as Mr Stone, and to give you a discount of, let's say, twenty-five percent? Would that be enough to tempt you back?"

"It's a very generous offer, Mr Roberts, but it would be extremely unfair to dump Luther. I've been very happy with the service he's provided." Plus, he was way hotter than Robert Roberts.

"I see." Mr Roberts frowned. "What if, hypothetically speaking, something was to happen to Mr Stone? If say, he was incapacitated in some way, and no longer able to provide you with accountancy services. How would you feel then?"

"I don't know."

"Think about it, Miss Gooder. One never knows what might happen, does one?"

With that, Robert Roberts turned on his heels, and walked out of my office. As soon as he'd left, Winky jumped onto my desk.

"That guy gives me the creeps." Winky shuddered.

"Me too."

Chapter 4

As I pulled onto my drive, I noticed a van parked on Megan's driveway. She'd obviously bought it for her new business venture, which she'd recently been discussing with Peter. The whole side of the van was covered with a huge picture of Megan, wearing a skimpy low-cut top, and ultra-short shorts. As always, she looked fantastic. In big, bold letters above her head, were the words 'Hot Plants.' The letter 'L' was in a smaller font than the other letters, so from a distance it looked as though it read 'Hot Pants.' It appeared that Peter now had competition.

I was still staring at the van when Megan's front door opened, and she came skipping out; she had a newspaper in her hand.

"What do you think, Jill?" She beamed. "Be honest. Do you like it?"

"It's—err—it's very nice. There's a lot of you on it, isn't there?"

"The guy who designed the artwork for the van seemed to think that having my picture on there would work best. I'm not sure why."

"It's hard to imagine."

"There's also a feature on my new business in today's Bugle." She handed me the newspaper. "I didn't think they'd be interested, but I spoke to a guy named Dougal Andrews, and he seemed very keen."

I just bet he did.

"You can keep that," she said. "I've got loads more copies in the house."

"Thanks. What's going to happen with the modelling?"

"I haven't given it up entirely because it'll take a while

to build up a customer base for the gardening business. I've told my agent to only book me out in the mornings. That leaves my afternoons free for the gardening. As I build up the new business, I'll gradually reduce the modelling assignments until I don't need them anymore."

"I'm really pleased for you, Megan. Best of luck with it."

"Thanks, Jill. You will tell Peter, won't you?"

"Oh yeah. I'll definitely tell Peter. In fact, I'll take a photo of your van, and send it to him."

Once inside, I emailed the photo to Peter, and then skimmed The Bugle's article on Megan. It was essentially just a large photo of her standing next to the van, and a few words about her new venture. The front-page headline was a little more interesting. *'Man found poisoned.'* Apparently, a man had been found dead in his apartment, having been poisoned by person or persons unknown.

The front door opened.

"Jack? Is that you?"

"Who else did you think it would be?" He walked through to the kitchen. "Have you seen the van next door?"

"I could hardly miss it?"

"Hot plants! Wow! Does Peter know yet?"

"I've just sent him a photo of the van—Kathy's going to love it. Anyway, what are you doing home so early?"

"I've got to go away on a residential course for four days."

"You didn't mention it."

"That's because the first I knew about it was an hour ago. The boss came to see me, and said that someone had dropped out. I wasn't supposed to go for another three months."

"When do you have to leave?"

"Tonight."

"Tonight? How long will you be gone for?"

"Four nights."

"That's just great!"

"Don't blame me." He pulled me close and gave me a kiss. "It's the job."

"I know, but what am I supposed to do while you're away?"

"Eat custard creams and watch TV?"

"Now you mention it, that does sound like a good idea. You should go away more often."

I made coffee, and we went through to the lounge.

"Where has it gone?" Jack said.

"Where's what gone?" I decided to play dumb.

"You know what. Where's my bowling trophy? The one I won with Megan."

Megan had partnered with Jack in a bowling competition, which by all accounts they'd won easily.

"It's enormous. It's too overpowering to be in this room, so I put it somewhere it wouldn't be quite so conspicuous."

"Where?"

"In the spare bedroom. On a chair, just inside the door."

"How is anyone meant to see my trophy if it's hidden away in the spare bedroom? Megan and I worked hard to win that. I want to keep it somewhere people can see it."

"Couldn't you take it to work with you?"

"I don't want it at work—I want it here."

"Okay. I'll bring it out the next time I'm up there." Unless of course I happened to forget. My memory wasn't what it used to be.

After dinner, I offered to do the dishes so that Jack could pack. After I'd finished, I took the rubbish outside to the dustbin.

"Hello, Jill," Mrs Rollo shouted over the fence.

We couldn't have wished for a nicer neighbour than Mrs Rollo. The only problem was that she loved to bake, and without exception, everything she made was practically inedible. I didn't like to say anything because I didn't want to hurt her feelings.

A young boy appeared at her side.

"This is Justin."

He had ginger hair and freckles, and his two front teeth were missing, so I couldn't make out if he was smiling or scowling at me.

"Justin's my grandson, Jill. He's staying with me today and tomorrow, aren't you Justin?"

"Yes, Grandma." He had a very high pitched voice.

"His mummy and daddy have gone to see Justin's auntie who isn't very well at the moment. I told them Justin could stay here with me."

"Hello, Justin," I said.

"Hello."

"Do you like staying with your grandma?"

"It's okay."

"I'm sure you'll have a great time."

"He will." Mrs Rollo hugged him to her. "He's such a good boy. Aren't you Justin? He's a little angel."

After seeing Jack off, I decided that I should treat myself to a glass of wine and a few of the chocolates I'd bought the night Jack had been bowling with Megan. I still had the bottom layer left. As I poured myself a glass of wine, I looked out onto the back garden at the bird bath. It was the one that I'd had at my old flat. I'd had to put it into storage when I'd been at Jack's place, but now we had our own house, I'd got it back.

Three sparrows were drinking and bathing when something spooked them, and they flew away. A few minutes later, another two sparrows perched on the bird bath, but within moments, something had spooked them too. This time I saw what had caused them to take flight. There was a tiny head peeping over Mrs Rollo's fence. It was Justin, and he was holding a catapult. What had she called him? Her little angel? Little monster, more like. How dare he fire his catapult at those innocent little birds?

I charged out of the back door, and down the garden. When I looked over the fence, there was no sign of Mrs Rollo, but Justin was still standing there.

"Excuse me, Justin."

"What?"

"You mustn't fire your catapult at the birds."

"Why not?"

"Because it's not a nice thing to do."

"It's funny."

"It's not funny. It's cruel."

"I haven't hit them yet."

"The bird bath is there for them to bathe and drink. I think you should give me that catapult."

"No." He took a step back.

"If you do it again I'll have to tell your grandma."

"Don't care."

What a horrible child he was. I walked back up the

garden until I was behind the shed, where I knew he wouldn't be able to see me.

I waited and watched.

A few minutes later, a blackbird perched on the bird bath, and began to take sips of water. Justin was pulling back the elastic on his catapult, so I quickly cast the 'illusion' spell, to make him see not a catapult but a snake, in his hand. The boy threw the catapult/snake onto the ground, and stared at it in horror. The snake started slithering towards him, so Justin turned tail and ran into the house. That would teach the little monster. Moments later Mrs Rollo emerged from the back door, holding Justin's hand.

"There are no snakes around here, Justin. You must be imagining things."

"But, Grandma, I saw it. It was in my hand."

"If you saw a snake, why did you pick it up? That's a silly thing to do."

"I didn't pick it up. I was holding my catapult, and it turned into a snake."

"What has your mummy told you about telling lies, Justin?"

"It's not a lie, Grandma. That's what happened. It was a catapult, and then it was a snake. Come and see." He led her down the garden. When he found the catapult lying on the ground, he stared at it in disbelief.

"The snake's gone," he said.

"What were you doing with that catapult, anyway?"

"Err—nothing."

"You know better than to play with those horrible things." She picked it up. "I'm confiscating this until you go back home, and I shall tell your mother that I do not approve of these."

After Mrs Rollo had taken the catapult back into the house, I stepped out from behind the shed, and called to Justin.

"That will teach you to be horrible to little birds, young man."

He scowled.

I'd no sooner got back into the house than someone knocked on the front door. It was Blake, the wizard who lived across the road.

"Are you okay, Blake?" He didn't look it—he looked rather drawn. "Do you want to come in?"

"Just for a minute. Jack's not in, is he?"

"No, he's had to go away for a few days on a course."

"Good. I was hoping to catch you by yourself."

"What is it? Is everything okay? Is Jen alright?"

"You remember I mentioned how difficult I've been finding it to keep my secret from Jen."

"Yeah?"

"I've decided I can't do it any longer. It's going to destroy our marriage. She still thinks I'm hiding something from her, and I can't think of any way to dispel her doubts other than to tell her the truth."

"Tell her that you're a wizard?"

"Yes."

"You mustn't do that, Blake. It's too dangerous. You know what will happen if word gets back to Candlefield. The Rogue Retrievers will come for you."

"I know, but what choice do I have? If I do nothing, sooner or later Jen is going to get fed up with the subterfuge, and leave me. At least this way I have a chance."

"But who's to say that Jen will believe you?"

"I might have to prove it to her. That's what other sups have done in my position. If I show her a few spells, I'm sure I can convince her, and then we can live together without this horrible black cloud hanging over us. It would mean that Jen will no longer suspect me of seeing someone else behind her back."

"I'm still not sure it's a good idea."

"I don't have any other option."

"When you tell her, you're not going to mention anything about me, are you?"

"Of course not. I shall just say that I'm a wizard."

"Well, I can't say I agree with your decision, but I wish you luck. Will you let me know how she reacts?"

"Yes, of course."

Chapter 5

Jack had trotted off to the Lake District for his residential course, leaving me on my lonesome. I'd just settled down to watch a movie when my phone beeped. It was a text message from Kathy:

'Don't forget to watch Wool TV tonight. I've got a new hairstyle. Let me know what you think of it.'

Great! So, instead of watching a blockbuster movie, I now had to endure Wool TV. This evening was just getting better and better. I could always pretend that I hadn't seen her text, but she'd know I was lying. But, then it occurred to me that I didn't need to watch the whole programme. As long as I saw Kathy's new hairstyle, then I'd be okay. I'd just have to hope that she didn't quiz me on the content of the programme.

When I tuned into Wool TV, I was a few minutes early, so I caught the news programme ahead of Kathy's regular spot. The news presenter was the 'famous' Lucinda Gray; the woman who Kathy had mentioned to me. The one she thought might be about to hand in her notice to pave the way for Kathy to take over as news anchor.

I had to admit that Lucinda Gray was a pro. She somehow managed to make yarn-related news at least somewhat interesting. After reading an article on the world-wide shortage of Blue Sapphire yarn, she took a quick sip of water from the glass on her desk. Then, without warning, she lurched forward, and collapsed face-down onto the desk. It took me a few moments to register what had happened. The screen went blank for a few seconds, and the next thing I knew, Kathy was on screen.

"Good evening, and welcome to Wool Talk, a little earlier than scheduled." She was obviously a little flustered, but her hair did look nice. It was shorter than she usually wore it.

Oh, well, I'd done my duty. I'd be able to tell her, hand on heart, that I'd seen her programme, and that I liked her hair.

***

What had I been thinking? Of all the films I could have chosen, I'd opted for a horror movie. I was hopeless when it came to watching them. It's not that they scared me, exactly. They just made me jump. I practically jumped off the sofa every time something unexpected happened. How was it that I routinely came into contact with real ghosts, vampires and werewolves, and none of those bothered me in the slightest, and yet here I was, hiding my face?

Just then, my phone rang, and I almost fell off the sofa.

"It's me," Kathy said.

"Hi. I thought your hair was—"

"Never mind my hair."

"What's the matter?"

"Did you see what happened to Lucinda?"

"I saw her collapse, but I thought you handled it like a pro."

"She's dead, Jill. Lucinda is dead."

"What? How?"

"No one knows. The police are here now. There are all kinds of rumours flying around."

"What kind of rumours?"

"That it could be murder."

"How?"

"I've no idea. Look, the reason I rang you is because I've been trying to get hold of Pete, but he's not answering his phone. Would you go around there and let him know what's happened? The police have said that we can't leave the building until they've spoken to everyone, so I've no idea what time I'm going to get home."

"Of course. Don't worry about it. I'll go straight over there. Keep me posted."

"Will do. I'd better go."

I jumped in the car, and drove to Kathy's house. Peter's car was on the driveway.

"Jill? Kathy's not in."

"I know. She asked me to come around and see you."

"Come in. Is she okay?"

"Yeah, she's fine. She's been trying to call you, but she said you weren't answering your phone."

He took his phone out of his pocket. "Five missed calls. I should have checked. I was at Tom Tom with Mikey; it's his practice day. I couldn't hear anything while he was banging those drums. What's going on?"

"There's been an incident at Wool TV, but Kathy's fine."

"What kind of incident?"

"Do you know the newsreader, Lucinda Gray?"

"I've never met her, but I've seen her on TV. Kathy mentioned she thought she might be looking for another job."

"She won't be now. She's dead."

"How?"

"It happened live on TV. I was watching Lucinda Gray reading the news, and suddenly she fell forward onto the desk. According to Kathy, it could be murder. Anyway, she asked me to tell you that the police have said that no one can leave until they've interviewed everyone, so she has no idea what time she'll get home."

"Okay. Thanks for coming over. Do you want a coffee or something?"

"Yeah, I might as well now that I'm here. Where are the kids?"

"Mikey's playing on his computer. Lizzie is in her room. I'm not sure what she's up to. She's been a little quiet since she got home from school."

"By the way, Peter, what did you make of Megan's van?"

He laughed. "It will certainly get her noticed."

"I don't think you have anything to worry about. Megan's nice enough, but how good a gardener is she?"

"She's certainly enthusiastic, and seems quite knowledgeable—except when it comes to moles."

After we'd finished our drinks, Peter took out his phone.

"I'm going to see if I can get hold of Kathy. Would you look in on Lizzie to see if she's okay?"

"Sure."

I knocked on Lizzie's door.

"Come in," a little voice squeaked.

Lizzie was lying on the bed, holding her teddy bear to her chest.

"Lizzie, are you okay?"

"Hello, Auntie Jill. Yeah, I'm okay."

"Are you sure? You look a little sad."

"I am a little bit, yes."

"Why is that?"

"My best friend, Katie, said she doesn't want to be my best friend anymore."

"Why not?"

"Because she wants to be best friends with Bethany."

"Couldn't she be best friends with both of you?"

"You can only have one best friend, Auntie Jill. Didn't you know that?"

"Yeah, sorry, of course. I wouldn't worry about it. I'm sure there are plenty of other people who you can be friends with."

"I do have other friends. I just don't have a best friend now, except for Joe."

"Who's Joe? Is he a boy in your class?"

"No." She managed a smile. "This is Joe—Joe Bear." She held up a tiny teddy bear, which looked like it had seen better days.

"I see."

"Joe has to be my best friend now because no one else wants to be."

I felt so sorry for Lizzie that I could have cried. It reminded me of my schooldays. I didn't have many friends, at least not compared to Kathy, who always had loads of friends around her.

Then, I had an idea. If Joe Bear was going to be Lizzie's best friend, then he should be able to talk to her. Since my visit to Aunt Lucy's, I'd been swotting up on 'enchantment' spells. This was my chance to put what I'd learned into action. When Lizzie wasn't looking, I cast the 'enchantment' spell which, if it worked properly, should mean that Joe Bear would be able to talk to her, but only her. No one else would know.

Peter and I watched TV, but neither of us could focus. We kept speculating on what might be happening with Kathy. Every time he'd tried to call her, it had gone to voicemail.

"I wouldn't worry." I tried to reassure him. "Kathy will be fine. She'll get in touch as soon as she can."

"I know."

About an hour later, Lizzie came out of her room, carrying Joe Bear. She had a broad smile on her face.

"I didn't know you were still here, Auntie Jill."

"I'm going to wait until your mummy gets home."

"Where is Mummy, Daddy?"

"She's had to work late tonight."

"Me and Joe would like something to eat, wouldn't we, Joe?" She looked lovingly at the bear. I was sure that he'd been talking to her, but he wouldn't do it now—not in front of other people.

"We'd like crisps and pop, please, Daddy."

"Okay. I'll bring it through to you."

"I don't know what you said to her," Peter said, after he'd taken Lizzie's crisps and drink through to her bedroom. "But you certainly managed to cheer her up."

Moments later, Kathy walked in. She looked tired and drawn.

"What's happened?" Peter took her hand.

"The police have confirmed that it's definitely murder. Poison, apparently." She took a seat on the sofa next to Peter.

"Do they have any idea who might have done it?" I said.

"I don't think so. I didn't like the policeman who was in charge."

"Was it Leo Riley?"

"Yeah, that's him. Is he Jack's replacement?"

"Yeah."

"He's a horrible man. I wish Jack was still over here. They took everyone's names and addresses, and said they'll be interviewing all of us in due course."

"What happens to Wool TV in the meantime?"

"I don't know. The station manager said he'd phone everyone tomorrow morning to let us know what's happening. All the programmes for the rest of the evening have been cancelled. I'm not sure whether we'll be on air tomorrow or not."

"They might ask you to read the news," I said.

"I don't know if I'd want to. I know I said I'd like Lucinda's job, but not this way. It just doesn't seem right."

Lizzie came rushing into the room. "Mummy! Mummy! I thought I heard you." She threw herself at Kathy. Kathy gave her a big hug, and a kiss on top of her head.

"I'm sorry I wasn't home earlier, pumpkin. I had to work late."

"That's okay, Mummy."

"How was your day at school?"

"Katie doesn't want to be my best friend anymore."

"Oh dear. How do you feel about that, pumpkin?"

"I don't mind. Katie's got a new best friend now, but I have too."

"That's good. Who's your new best friend?"

"Joe Bear."

"Oh?" Kathy looked surprised. "That's nice."

"Joe can talk to me now."

"The bear talks to you?"

"Yes. He's been telling me stories."

"You'd better get off back to bed now. I'll come and kiss you goodnight in a few minutes."

"Okay, Mummy." Lizzie ran back to her bedroom.

"Oh dear." Kathy sighed. "She and Katie were such good friends."

"She seems to have taken it well," I said.

"I know. I thought she'd be more upset."

"The bear seems to have cheered her up."

"I guess so, but I'm not sure how I feel about her having a teddy bear as a best friend. It's a bit sad, isn't it?"

Chapter 6

It was the next morning, and the house felt empty without Jack. I hadn't slept particularly well, but at least I hadn't had a repeat of that horrible nightmare where I'd been chasing Aunt Lucy along corridors.

I was halfway through breakfast when there was a knock at the door. Who on earth was it at that time of day?

The man was quite obviously a wizard. He was dressed in a most unusual blue uniform. On his hat and breast pocket, he had identical badges—the letters CSD with an arrow through them.

"Are you Jill Gooder?"

"I am."

"Good. I have the right address. I'm Laurence Waters, but all my friends call me Puddle. I work for Candlefield Special Delivery." He tapped the badge on his breast pocket.

"You're a postman?"

"Kind of, I suppose. We deliver letters and parcels from the sup world to the human world." He pulled a letter out of the small bag he was carrying. "This is for you."

"Thank you."

"My pleasure. Have a good day." And with that, he hurried back down the drive.

A special delivery from Candlefield? Who could that be from? Perhaps the Combined Sup Council had sent it, but then they usually left messages with Aunt Lucy. I went back into the kitchen, took a sip of my coffee, and opened the envelope which had a watermark on it: the letters CASS. The sheet of paper inside had the same watermark, and a letterhead which read: 'Candlefield Academy of Supernatural Studies.'

The letter, which was handwritten, was from a Desdemona Nightowl, headmistress at Candlefield Academy of Supernatural Studies. It was an invitation for me to give a talk at the school. The gist of it was that the school was keen for their pupils to learn as much about humans as possible. I was the closest thing to a human they were likely to get because humans could never go to Candlefield.

I wasn't sure what to make of it. I could understand why they'd chosen me because, although I wasn't a human, I'd lived as one for over twenty years. It was an honour to be asked, but also a little scary.

There was a cut-off slip at the bottom, so that I could RSVP. I didn't want to make any snap decisions because it was a big responsibility. I knew absolutely nothing about Candlefield Academy of Supernatural Studies, but it occurred to me that Aunt Lucy might, so after breakfast, I magicked myself over there.

Much to my surprise, Aunt Lucy was standing in front of her house, looking up and down the street. She looked distraught.

"Aunt Lucy? What's the matter?"

"It's Matilda."

"Matilda? Oh, yes, your lawnmower. What about her?"

"The 'enchantment' spell must have been too strong. It appears to have given her an insatiable appetite for grass."

"How do you mean?"

"It seems she needs a regular intake of it. My small lawn

isn't enough to satisfy her. She's mown it five times in the last two days; there's barely a blade of grass left on there. Now she's gone in search of other grass. I don't know where she is, Jill. She just disappeared down the street."

"Couldn't you get Grandma or another level six witch to reverse the enchantment?"

"I've tried contacting your grandmother, but as always, whenever you need her, she's nowhere to be found. Can't you do something?"

"But I'm still only on level four. I'm not sure I could reverse a level six enchantment."

"You're the most powerful witch in Candlefield. If anyone can do it, you can. Look! There she is. Do you see her? Down there on the left! She's mowing Teresa Bodangle's lawn."

A woman, who I took to be the aforementioned Teresa Bodangle, was standing in the doorway staring at the lawnmower, and no doubt wondering what was going on. It didn't take Matilda long to finish up. After she had, she came charging out of the garden, onto the pavement, and down to the next house where she started on that lawn. This was getting out of hand.

"Please, Jill, you need to stop her." Aunt Lucy sounded desperate. "What will my neighbours think if Matilda ruins their lawns?"

"Okay. I'll see what I can do."

I set off in pursuit of the errant lawnmower, but had only gone a few paces when I saw her come out of the second garden. She'd finished already, and was headed off down the road. A few moments later, she disappeared through yet another gateway. I crossed the road, and as I got closer, I realised she was now in Candlefield Bowling

Club. If she ruined their bowling green, there'd be hell to pay. I reached the gate just as Matilda was about to jump onto the grass.

I'd never had to reverse an 'enchantment' spell before, so I was going to have to improvise with a spell of my own. If it didn't work, the bowling green would be ruined.

I cast the spell, and hoped for the best.

Matilda stopped dead in her tracks.

"What's going on?" It was a wizard with a long moustache. "What's this lawnmower doing in here?"

"Sorry. It was a bit of a misunderstanding. There's no harm done. See, it hasn't started to cut the grass."

He glanced down. "A good job too. Do you know how much it costs us to keep this bowling green in this condition?"

"An awful lot, I imagine."

"Indeed. Is this your mower?"

"Kind of."

"In that case, I would suggest you get it out of here immediately."

I pushed Matilda out of the gate, and up the road. By the time I got back to Aunt Lucy's, I was exhausted.

"Thanks, Jill. When I saw Matilda go into the bowling club, I thought we were in real trouble. Did you manage to stop her in time?"

"Yes. She didn't do any damage. I'm sorry, but I had to override the 'enchantment' spell. Matilda's never going to be able to mow your lawn unaided again."

"Don't worry about that. I've learned my lesson. I'll do it the hard way from now on. It's not worth all this aggravation." Aunt Lucy put Matilda back into the shed, and we went inside for a cup of tea.

Before I had the chance to ask her about the invitation I'd received, the twins arrived. As soon as they walked through the door, it was obvious that something was wrong. They weren't their usual bubbly selves. In fact, they seemed very subdued.

"What's the matter with you two?" Aunt Lucy said. "I hope you haven't been falling out with your husbands again."

"No, of course we haven't, Mum." Amber joined me at the kitchen table.

"Why do you always think that?" Pearl took the seat next to Amber. "If you must know, we seem to be losing customers at Cuppy C."

"How do you mean, losing them?" I asked.

"The numbers are down. Dramatically down," Amber said. "We're only getting about half the number of people through the door that we normally get."

Aunt Lucy poured them both a cup of tea, and then joined us at the table.

"Have there been any complaints or problems?"

"No. That's just it." Amber took a sip of tea. "Nothing like that. Everything seems to be fine, but the numbers are definitely down. We have a lot of regulars, who usually come in once or twice a week, but we haven't seen them for ages. I don't know what's going on."

"Presumably, the takings are down too?" Aunt Lucy said.

"That's what we don't understand." Pearl shook her head. "Although we're definitely getting fewer people through the door, the takings are as good as ever. In fact, a couple of days have been better than average."

"You mentioned that the other day when I came in," I said. "You thought Amber had miscounted."

"She did say that, didn't she?" Amber chimed in. "And had I, Pearl?"

"No, I was wrong," Pearl admitted. "Her figures were correct, and it's happened again since then. The money's holding up, and yet we're losing customers. It doesn't make any sense."

"Could I have some toast, Mum?" Amber said.

"I suppose so. Do you all want some?"

We all nodded.

While we were all eating toast and strawberry jam, I took the opportunity to ask about the invitation I'd received.

"Do any of you know about Candlefield Academy of Supernatural Studies?"

"CASS? It's Candlefield's most prestigious school," Aunt Lucy said.

"Prestigious how? Do you mean expensive?"

"No, it's actually free to attend, but admission is by invitation only. The very best wizards and witches are invited to attend. You can't apply, and there are no entrance exams."

"How do they know which kids will turn out to be the best witches or wizards?"

"Nobody knows how they determine who to invite, but their track record suggests they get it right more often than not."

"We didn't get an invite." Amber sounded quite indignant.

"No, we didn't," Pearl said. "But I wouldn't have wanted to go there anyway. It's a boarding school. Ugh!

Can you imagine having to live at your school? I wouldn't have liked that. I was always glad to come home after school had finished for the day."

"Me too." Amber nodded.

"If you'd been living in Candlefield as a child, Jill, I'm absolutely convinced that you would have been invited to attend CASS," Aunt Lucy said.

"Definitely," Pearl agreed. "But would you have wanted to go there, Jill? How would you have felt about being a boarder?"

"I don't know. It's not something I've ever thought about. Where I grew up, everyone went to the local school. There was no other choice. Boarding schools are always made to seem exciting in books and movies, but I'm not sure they would be in real life. Can you imagine, when you were a kid, not getting to see your mum and dad until the end of each term?"

"What made you ask about CASS, anyway?" Aunt Lucy said.

I took the invitation out of my pocket. "This came this morning by Candlefield Special Delivery. It's an invitation for me to give a talk there. They want someone to talk about what it's like to be a human, but for obvious reasons, they can't actually invite a human."

"You should definitely do it," Aunt Lucy said. "It would do them good to get your perspective on what humans are like. Some sups have absolutely no idea."

"You don't for a start, Mum," Amber said. "You've hardly ever been to the human world."

"I know, but I read a lot."

"That hardly counts." Pearl snatched half a slice of toast from Amber's plate.

"So, are you going to do it, Jill?" Amber snatched it back.

"I don't know. Where is the school, anyway? I've never noticed it when I've been walking around Candlefield."

"It's hardly surprising you haven't seen it," Aunt Lucy said. "It's way up north; on the very edge of the sup world. The only way to get there is by air-ship."

"Seriously? I've never seen an air-ship in the skies above Candlefield."

"They only fly back and forth to CASS. And the only time they run is at the start and end of the school term."

"Couldn't I just magic myself there?"

"You could try, but I wouldn't recommend it. The school is surrounded by thick forests and mountains. Trying to get a 'lock' on the school would be like trying to find a needle in a haystack. Even if you only got it slightly wrong, you could end up stuck high in a giant tree, or land smack bang in a raging river. You might even end up in a dragon's nest. That wouldn't be fun."

"Dragon? The only dragon I've ever seen was at the Levels Competition."

"The Destroyer Dragon?"

"Yeah. That was it. Horrible thing."

"Where do you think that came from?"

"I seem to remember someone mentioned that it normally lived on the very edge of the sup world."

"That's right. And it has lots of friends up there."

"How come I haven't seen any more of them down here?"

"Those creatures have always lived in the far north. The habitat there suits them. Why do you think sups chose to live in the south?"

"No scary creatures?"

"Precisely."

"This is sounding less and less appealing. I don't know what to do."

"You should ask Daze about CASS," Amber said.

"Yeah." Pearl was now eyeing my last piece of toast. "Daze went to CASS."

"Really? In that case, I'll get the lowdown from her before I make my mind up."

Chapter 7

I magicked myself back to Washbridge. Jules was behind the desk, and she didn't look very happy.

"Morning, Jules."

"Morning, Jill." She managed a smile. Barely.

"Something tells me that you and Jethro are having problems."

"I'm really annoyed with him. He says he wants to start dancing again in one of those horrible dance troupes."

"I take it you don't want him to?"

"Of course I don't. Have you seen them?"

I nodded. I'd once been dragged to see an all-male dance troupe by Mad.

"I don't want him showing off his body to all the other women in Washbridge."

"And you've told him this, I assume?"

"I told him that if he insists on going ahead with it, I may have to finish with him."

"And what did he say to that?"

"Nothing really, so I don't know whether he's going to do it or not."

I went through to my office, where I found Winky walking slowly across the room on his back legs. He was balancing a book on his head. I must have made him jump because the book fell to the floor.

"That was your fault." He turned on me. "Why didn't you knock?"

"This is my office! Why should I have to knock?"

"In case someone happens to be practising their deportment skills."

I collapsed onto the sofa, laughing so hard that my sides

hurt.

He sighed. "And what, may I ask is so funny about that?"

"You mean apart from the fact that there's a cat in my office trying to balance a book on his head? Nothing much, I guess."

He picked up the book, and threw it across the room. "I hate to admit it, but you're right. This is ridiculous. It's not like I walk on my back legs very often, so why do I need to go through this torture?"

"Because you love Bella, and there's nothing you wouldn't do to make her happy."

"You're enjoying this way too much."

A few minutes later, Winky had given up on the deportment exercises, and was tucking into a bowl of tuna mix.

What? I can't afford salmon every day.

My phone rang. It was Peter, and I knew as soon as he spoke that something was wrong.

"Jill, it's Kathy."

"What about her? Is she okay?"

"No. Yes. I don't know."

"Take a breath. What's going on?"

"She's been taken in for questioning about the Lucinda Gray murder."

"She? What? Why?" Now I was the one who was struggling to speak coherently. "What do you mean? As a witness?"

"They're treating her as though she's a suspect. I asked if I could go with her, but they wouldn't let me. Luckily, the kids were already at school so they didn't see anything. I don't know what to do."

"Leave it with me. Let me call Jack. He should be able to find out what's going on."

"Okay, thanks. You'll let me know, won't you?"

"Of course."

I immediately called Jack. He didn't answer on the first three attempts, but on the fourth one, he picked up.

"What's wrong? I couldn't answer before because I was in class. Is there a problem?"

"It's Kathy."

"What's happened to her?"

"She's been taken in for questioning about the murder of Lucinda Gray, the newsreader. Peter just rang me. He says they're treating her as though she's a suspect. I need you to find out what's going on."

"How am I meant to do that? I'm in the Lake District."

"Come on, Jack. This is my sister we're talking about. Make a call."

"Okay. Leave it with me. I'll see what I can find out."

I heard the outer office door crash open, and moments later, Grandma came marching in, red faced—the wart on the end of her nose was glowing. This definitely wasn't a social call.

Winky jumped off the sofa, and hid underneath it, as he always did when Grandma came around.

"Morning, Grandma."

"Where's that sister of yours? She promised me that her TV work wouldn't interfere with her job at Ever A Wool Moment. So, where is she this morning? Not in my shop, that's for sure."

"Hold on, Grandma, Kathy's been taken in for questioning. She's a suspect in a murder case."

"What kind of excuse is that?"

I could hardly believe my ears. "It's not an excuse. It's a fact. She's currently at Washbridge police station."

"Well, that's all very inconvenient. I've got a shop full of customers and no one to serve them. It's not as though I don't already have enough to contend with, what with all those stupid fish, crabs and seahorses wandering around the street, blocking the view of my shop. Don't you think it's stressful enough for me without having to serve customers?"

I was beyond angry. Grandma could push me further than I thought possible.

"My sister is a suspect in a murder case! I think that is slightly more important than your retail problems."

"You would. That's why your business is in the state it's in. What's happened with Kathy, exactly?"

"I don't know. I've phoned Jack. He's going to try to find out. As soon as I know anything, I'll let you know, but I doubt you'll see her today."

"Great! It looks like I'll have to do everything myself, as per usual. But first, I'm going to sort out those stupid fish people across the road."

"Hold on, Grandma. Are you talking about using magic on them?"

"Of course I am. I'll shrink them to the size of a termite; they won't block my shop window then."

"No, don't do that! I know the woman who owns the shop."

"You do? How?"

"She used to live in the same apartment block as me. She worked as a tax inspector back then."

"That explains a lot."

"Let me have a word with her before you do anything rash. I'll see if I can talk her into moving the fish, crab and seahorse away from your premises."

"Okay. But if they're not gone within a couple of hours, I will take matters into my own hands."

And with that, she stormed out of the office.

Such a caring individual, my grandmother.

Ten minutes later, Jack rang back.

"I've tried to talk to Leo Riley, but he won't even take my call. I had to call in a few favours from some of my old colleagues. The reason they took her in for questioning is because they found the syringe that was used to inject poison into Lucinda Gray's water bottle, in Kathy's drawer at the TV station."

"What?" I couldn't believe my ears. "Kathy could never do anything like that. And even if she had, the last thing she'd do would be to leave the syringe in her drawer where anyone could find it."

"I agree."

"It's obviously been planted there. What can we do about it, Jack?"

"According to the people I spoke to, they're expecting Kathy to be released later today, or tomorrow at the latest."

"But what about the real murderer? I wouldn't trust Leo Riley to find a shoelace in a shoe cupboard."

"You mustn't get involved, Jill. Kathy will be released soon. Do you promise?"

"Okay. I'll wait until she's home."

It was time to pay a visit to She Sells to have a chat with

Betty Longbottom. She had to stop those promotional characters from standing outside Ever a Wool Moment. If she didn't, Grandma would no doubt let loose her magic on them, and maybe on Betty too.

"Jules, I'm just going to nip down to—"

Before I could finish the sentence, the door opened, and in walked two women wrapped in towels. They looked around, obviously a little confused. The one with the gammy toe spoke.

"Is this the sauna?"

"Does it look like a sauna?" I snapped.

"Not really."

"These are my offices. I'm Jill Gooder, private investigator."

"The brochure said there was a sauna."

"Would that have been the I-Sweat brochure, by any chance?"

"Yeah. Me and Pauline are on the free month's trial, but if there isn't a sauna, I don't think we'll be signing up."

"I-Sweat may well have a sauna, but like I said before, this is my office."

"Do you know where the sauna is, then?"

"I imagine it's back along the corridor—where you just came from."

"What about sunbeds? Have you got any of them?"

"No. No sunbeds, and no sauna."

"You're sure?"

"Positive."

"That's the third time this week that's happened," Jules said, after gammy toe and her friend had left.

"Are you kidding?"

"No. Two of them wanted the sauna, and the other one

was looking for the masseuse."

"I'll have to have a word with the I-Sweat guys, and get them to improve their signage. Anyway, as I was saying, I'm going to nip down the road to that new shop, She Sells."

"It's a weird kind of a shop, isn't it? They only seem to sell seashells and stuff. What's the point of that? Who would want to buy those?"

"You'd be surprised. Apparently, there's a thriving trade in seashells and the like."

As I made my way down the high street, I could see why Grandma was annoyed. The giant marine characters were patrolling both sides of the street; three of them were congregated in front of Ever, completely blocking the window.

There were a surprising number of customers inside She Sells. At first, I didn't think Betty was in there, but then I spotted her at the back.

"Betty, could I have a word?"

"Hello again, Jill. Are you looking for some seashells for your new house?"

"Not today. I just wanted a quick word. I don't know if you're aware, but my grandmother owns the shop across the road." I pointed.

"Ever A Wool Moment?"

"That's right."

"I've never really liked that name," she said.

"Me neither. I suggested Stitch Slapped, but Grandma didn't go for it. Anyway, she's a little unhappy about your promotional people congregating outside there. They're blocking the view of the window, and she feels it might affect trade."

"I don't want to upset your grandmother, but business is business, and this promotion is working particularly well. We need to cover both sides of the street to maximize the effect."

"Couldn't they just move up the street a little rather than standing outside Ever?"

"The thing is, if they catch potential customers right there, it's easier for them to point to She Sells. We're smack bang across the road from Ever A whatsit."

"I think you'd be well-advised to get them to move along. You really don't want to upset my grandmother or you may live to regret it."

Betty laughed. "I'm sorry, Jill, but as you know, I worked as a tax inspector for several years, so I'm used to handling difficult people. I'm sure I can cope with your grandmother."

The poor deluded fool.

"Okay, Betty." I sighed. "Don't say I didn't warn you."

When I got back, there was a young man waiting in the outer office.

"He doesn't have an appointment," Jules said. "I told him I wasn't sure if you'd be able to see him or not, but he said you knew him, and that he'd like to wait."

Knew him? I looked a little closer, and then it clicked. It was Norman, a.k.a. Mastermind, who I'd first encountered working in a prop shop. His uncle's prop shop, to be precise. The next time I'd come across him was when he'd been going out with Betty Longbottom. But what was he doing here?

"Norman? Nice to see you again. Come through to my

office."

He did a double-take at Winky.

"That cat's only got one eye."

Nothing got past Mastermind.

"What brings you here, Norman?"

"I've got a problem." Never had a truer word been spoken.

"What's that?"

"My bottle tops have gone missing."

I'd almost forgotten about Norman's collection of bottle tops. When he and Betty had been an item, she'd told me that he collected them.

"Do you mean you've misplaced them?"

"No. Somebody's nicked 'em."

"Who would want to steal your bottle tops?"

"Bottle tops are big business. I know most people think it's just a stupid hobby, but the rare ones are very sought after. I should know; I've spent my life studying them."

"Okay. I'll take your word for that."

"There's a lot of rivalry in the bottle top world."

"Really?"

"Toppers—that's what they call people who collect bottle tops—will do anything to get their hands on the rare ones."

"Have you reported the theft?"

"Yeah, I've told the police, but they don't seem very interested. That's why I thought of you. I remembered you were a private investigator, so I thought you might be able to find 'em for me."

"My fees may be more than you can afford, just to find a few bottle tops."

"Money's not a problem. I sold one of my best tops only

the other day."

"How much did you get for it?"

"Ten grand."

"Ten thousand pounds for one bottle top?"

"Yeah, but it was the Blue Diamond. There were only fifteen ever made. I didn't want to sell it, but I needed the cash, so it had to go."

"Right, and do you have any other bottle tops that are worth that kind of money?"

"Lots of 'em."

"Really?"

"Well, I don't actually have 'em now, because somebody's nicked 'em. Can you find 'em, or what?"

"I can certainly try. Can you give me the names of all your rivals, and anyone else that you think may have been involved?"

"I've wrote it all down, here." He took a scruffy piece of paper from his pocket. "There you go. It'll definitely be one of them on that list."

Chapter 8

I was just about to call it a day and go home, when I got another call from Peter. He sounded a lot calmer now.

"Jill, I just thought I should let you know that Kathy's home."

"Is she okay? Can I speak to her?"

"She's still upset. It might be best to let her rest."

"I'm going to come around."

I drove straight over there.

"Where is she?"

"She's having a lie-down in the bedroom. I think she's asleep." Peter looked like he could do with some sleep himself.

"Where are the kids?"

"The neighbours have taken them for a couple of hours."

"Do the neighbours know what's happened?"

"Yeah, but they won't say anything. They're good people."

As we made our way into the lounge, Kathy appeared.

"I thought you were having a nap," Peter said.

"I can't sleep." Her hair was dishevelled, and she'd obviously been crying.

"I'll make us a drink," Peter offered.

Kathy and I sat on the sofa together, and I took her hand in mine.

"Are you okay?"

"Not really. I can't believe they think I could have murdered her."

"No one with half a brain would. It's that stupid Leo Riley. The man's an idiot."

"I've never seen that syringe before. I've no idea how it got into the drawer in my desk. Somebody is obviously trying to frame me." She blew her nose. "Sorry, I'm just feeling sorry for myself. It's Lucinda I should be feeling sorry for. She didn't deserve to die like that. Would you investigate this, Jill?"

"Of course I will, but you're going to have to give me as much information as you can."

"About Lucinda? To be honest, I didn't know her that well. She was the star; I'm just the newbie. We'd made small talk a few times, but that was about it. The person that you really need to speak to is her PA, Donna Proudlove. She and Lucinda were really close. I got the impression they were friends as well as work colleagues. She'll be able to tell you as much about Lucinda as anyone."

"Okay, I'll see if I can get a hold of Donna, tomorrow."

I stayed with Kathy for the best part of two hours. She was quiet for a lot of that time, and I allowed her to be. Peter kept reassuring her that everything was going to be okay. I knew she was in good hands with Peter.

On my way home, I picked up a copy of The Bugle which had the headline: *'Washbridge poisoner strikes again!'*

The article linked Lucinda's murder with the one from a few days earlier. It said that the MO in both cases was the same: Poison had been injected into a bottle of water. I had no way of knowing how accurate the article was—this was The Bugle, after all. It might have been no more than speculation on their part, but it was also possible they had someone on the inside, at Washbridge police station, who was feeding them information in return for a nice backhander.

When I arrived home, there was a car on Mrs Rollo's drive. Mrs Rollo, her little monster of a grandson, Justin, and another woman came out of her house. I tried to get inside before they saw me, but I was too slow.

Mrs Rollo called, "Come on over and meet my daughter."

Drat it! So near, and yet so far.

I put on a smile, and walked around there.

"This is my daughter, Sheila. Sheila Thyme."

Sheila's hair looked as though it had been forged in steel, and lowered onto her head. There wasn't a hair out of place.

"And, you must be Jill," she with the perfect hair said. "My mother's told me a lot about you. You're a private investigator, I believe?"

"That's right."

"That must be really exciting."

"It can be sometimes."

"I'm here to collect Justin. Mum's been looking after him for me. He's such a little treasure, aren't you?" She pulled Justin close to her. "Such an angel."

Angel? That little monster had been trying to kill the birds on my bird bath with his catapult.

Justin stuck out his tongue at me—unseen by his mother.

"Have you tasted any of my mother's baking, Jill?"

"Err—yeah, your mum often gives us buns and cakes." Unfortunately.

"They're jolly good, aren't they?"

"Yeah, very nice."

I couldn't make my mind up whether Sheila Thyme genuinely believed her mother could bake, or if she was just winding me up.

"I've persuaded Mum to enter the Washbridge Annual Baking Competition. She's bound to win, don't you think?"

I was so stunned, I could barely speak. There was more chance of Winky winning the Washbridge Annual Baking Competition than of Mrs Rollo winning it. Not only were most of her cakes inedible, they looked monstrous as well. She'd be a laughing stock if she entered.

"I imagine there'll be some tough competition."

"Don't worry about that." Sheila waved away my concerns. "Mum will win, for sure."

She was obviously high on something.

***

Later that evening, I was on the phone to Jack.

"How's Kathy?"

"Back home. I called in after work. She's upset, understandably—scared more than anything else. I promised her that I'll investigate the murder."

"Is there any point in my telling you to keep out of it, or would I be wasting my breath?"

"What do you think?"

"I'll save my breath, then. Just try to keep out of Leo Riley's way. You don't need any aggro from him, and *I* certainly don't."

"Don't worry, Jack. I'll be discretion itself."

For some reason, that made him laugh.

"How's the course?"

"Boring, but then it seems like every course I've ever been on is boring. They're either not relevant, or they're telling their grandmother how to suck eggs."

"Who does that?"

"Who does what?

"Suck eggs."

"I don't know. It's just a saying."

"Still, seems like a funny thing to— "

"Jill! Focus!"

"Sorry. What were you saying?"

"That I'll be glad when the course is over. Not long to go now. I'm missing you."

"Good."

"That's where you're supposed to say that you're missing me too."

"Of course I am. Hey, you'll never guess what happened tonight?"

"You polished my bowling trophy, and put it in pride of place on the mantelpiece?"

"Close. I bumped into Mrs Rollo. She had her daughter and grandson with her. Her daughter has apparently persuaded Mrs Rollo to enter the Washbridge Annual Baking Competition."

Jack laughed. "That's a joke, I assume."

"No, I'm deadly serious."

"Why would she persuade her to enter a baking competition? The woman can't bake to save her life."

"I know, but her daughter seems to think she can."

"It's going to be very embarrassing for her. I feel sorry for the poor woman. Anyway, I'd better go. I promised I'd have a drink with some of the guys."

"Is that *guys* as in men, or *guys* as in men and women?"

"A mix of both. You've got nothing to worry about, though. I only have eyes for you."

"It's not your eyes I'm worried about."

I'd just settled down for an evening's viewing when there was a knock at the door. It was Blake, and I could see he was upset.

"What's the matter?"

"Can I come in?"

"Of course. Come through to the lounge. What's happened?"

"I took the plunge. I did it."

"Did what?"

"I've told Jen that I'm a wizard."

"What happened?"

"It didn't go well. She reacted badly. She thought I was just making up a stupid story to cover up something else."

"I thought she trusted you now."

"It's my own stupid fault. I think I've just gone and stirred it all up again. I don't know what to do."

"Where is she now?"

"In the house. I told her I was going out to the shop. I needed to talk it through with you. As far as I can see, I have only two options. I can either cast the 'forget' spell and make her forget everything I've just told her, or I can show her some magic to prove to her that I'm a wizard. Then she'd have to believe me."

"I wouldn't do that, Blake. I think you're on very dodgy ground. One wrong word, and the Rogue Retrievers will take you back to Candlefield, and that would be the end of your marriage. You don't want that, do you?"

"No, of course not."

"If I was you, I'd get back there as quickly as I could, and cast the 'forget' spell and hope that it works this time."

"It didn't work the last time I used it, if you remember."

"You've still got to try, and if that doesn't work, just tell her you were joking, and apologise for upsetting her."

"I'm still tempted to show her some magic."

"You'll regret it."

He got up, and I showed him to the door.

"Don't do anything rash, Blake."

"I won't, I promise."

I'd no sooner sat down than there was another knock at the door. Was I ever going to get any peace tonight? I assumed it must be Blake back again. Maybe he'd tried the 'forget' spell and it had failed.

It was a woman. She was dressed in a long purple cape, and was holding a walking stick.

"I'm sorry to call on you unannounced. I'm Desdemona Nightowl—Headmistress of Candlefield Academy of Supernatural Studies. Can you spare me a few moments of your time?"

"Of course. Please come in. Can I get you a drink?"

"Not for me. There's somewhere else I need to be shortly, so I'll get straight to the point. I wondered if you'd had the chance to consider our invitation to speak at the school?"

She placed her walking stick on the floor. It had a silver top in the shape of a dragon's head.

"I've been giving it a lot of thought."

"And have you made a decision?"

I'd hoped to have the chance to speak to Daze before deciding whether to give the talk or not, but as this woman had come all this way, I felt I owed it to her to let her have my answer now. Should I or shouldn't I? The school sounded fascinating, but those dragons sounded scary. Yes? No?

"Yes. I'd be honoured to accept your invitation." Had I just said that out loud?

"Wonderful! That's excellent news. One of my major concerns is the high number of young sups who move to the human world. I'm particularly worried about our own alumni. I feel that the best brains of the sup world are being lost to the human world. I hope your speech might, in some way, influence them to stay in Candlefield."

"I didn't realise that was what you had in mind. I thought you just wanted me to explain what it's like to be human, as best I can."

"Indeed I do, but I'm hoping that you'll also let them know that the human world is not some kind of paradise—that it has its faults too. That way, hopefully, our pupils will at least think twice before making the decision to move there."

"I'm quite happy to tell them there are pros and cons to living here, but surely you're not asking me to exaggerate or lie about the cons?"

"No, of course not, Miss Gooder. I would never ask you to do that. Just be honest and tell them about any problems that you've encountered living as a sup in the human world."

"Okay, I can do that. When exactly did you want me to give the talk?"

"We have a few other events coming up on the calendar, but I'm hoping to clear a date sometime next month, if that suits?"

"That's fine."

"Once we've sorted out a date, I'll send you more details, including a ticket for the air-ship. It normally only runs at the start and end of term, but special arrangements can be made, just as they were for my visit tonight."

Chapter 9

The next morning, when I stepped out of the door, Jen was just coming out of her house. Blake's car had already gone, so I knew she was by herself. I hoped I might get to my car without her spotting me, but she beckoned me over.

This wasn't going to be an easy conversation.

"Jill, do you have a minute?"

"I was just on my way to work, so it'll have to be quick."

"I only need a minute. Can we go inside, though? I don't really want to talk about this out here."

I followed her into the house.

"Is something wrong, Jen?" As if I didn't already know the answer to that question.

"After I had you follow Blake for me, I felt much more reassured that I'd been imagining things, and that he wasn't hiding anything from me. But then I started to have doubts again. And after last night, I don't know what to think."

"What happened last night?"

"This is going to sound insane, but just hear me out. Blake said he wanted to come clean. I honestly thought he was going to say he'd been having an affair, and in a way, it might have been easier if he had. At least that would've made sense. But that's not what he told me." She hesitated. "You're going to think I've lost my mind."

"Go on. You may as well tell me now."

"He told me he's a wizard."

"A wizard?" I forced a weak laugh.

"I know. It's crazy, but that's what he said. He sat me

down and told me that he wasn't a human, but a wizard. I just laughed at him. I thought it was some sort of joke, but he was deadly serious. Then he went on to say that he came from another land; a land where supernaturals live. Apparently, the supernaturals, or sups as he called them, can live in the human world, but humans can't go there. Now, you tell me, Jill, what am I meant to make of that rubbish?"

"Maybe he was joking, and took it too far. How did things end up?"

"While he was out at the shop, I went to bed. I couldn't handle anymore. I thought we could talk about it this morning, but when I woke up, he'd gone. I probably should have just laughed it off, and left it at that. What do you think?"

"I honestly don't know."

"Surely, you don't believe in wizards and supernatural stuff, do you?"

"Me? No, of course not."

"I'm sorry, Jill. I shouldn't have wasted your time. I know you want to get to work. Thanks for listening to me."

"No problem, Jen. Any time."

Oh boy!

***

I'd arranged to meet with Donna Proudlove, Lucinda Gray's PA, in a coffee shop called Coffee Spotty. It turned out that its actual name was Coffee Spot, but some kind individual had helpfully added 'TY' to the end of the sign. The coffee shop was only a few doors down from the TV studios where Wool TV was recorded.

Donna was in her mid-twenties, tall, with cropped blonde hair.

"Thanks for seeing me, Donna."

"That's okay. If there's anything I can do to help, I'll be more than happy to. Lucinda was more than just a boss to me; she was my friend. When I applied for this position there were dozens of applicants. I didn't think I stood a chance because I was straight out of uni, and had hardly any experience. I'd worked in university TV, but that was all. When Lucinda gave me the job, I asked her why she'd chosen me. She said she wanted someone who came to it fresh, and not with preconceived ideas learned from other TV stations." Donna hesitated. "This is going to sound terrible."

"Go on," I prompted.

"I'm devastated by Lucinda's death, and obviously, I want whoever did it to be brought to justice, but I'm also worried for my own future. Is that selfish of me?"

"No, it's perfectly understandable."

"It's just that I don't know who's going to take her job. Whoever it is will probably want to bring in their own people. If I lose this job, I'm not sure I'll get another one."

"I'm sure you'll be fine. You worked for Lucinda Gray—that will look good on your CV. Look, Donna, before we go any further, I think it's only fair I tell you that I'm Kathy's sister. She presents the weekly magazine feature on Wool TV."

"Kathy? Yeah, I know her. I heard that she was a suspect, and had been taken in for questioning."

"She was, yes, but she's been released now."

"Kathy would no more murder someone than I would.

Is that why you're investigating this?"

"Yeah. She's asked me to see what I can uncover."

"Is there anything I can do?"

"Answering my questions is help enough. Did Lucinda act any differently on the days leading up to her death? Was there anything that seemed to be bothering her?"

"No. She seemed her usual self."

"Kathy mentioned that she thought Lucinda might be moving to a different job with another TV station."

"Lucinda and I were very close, but she didn't tell me everything. She hadn't mentioned another job to me."

"Who else was close to Lucinda? Is there anyone else you think I should talk to?"

"You should probably start with her ex-husband, Michael Gray. Lucinda kept his name after they were divorced. From all accounts, he was very bitter about the way the marriage ended. I don't really know him; I've only met him a couple of times. And then there's her new boyfriend. She'd been seeing a guy called Callum Hamilton. I don't like him very much. He's a model, very good-looking, and quite a bit younger than Lucinda. He really fancies himself. He's modelled jumpers and the like on Wool TV a few times. That's how they met. You might also want to speak to Lucinda's sister, Audrey Bone. Lucinda didn't talk about her very often, but from what I could gather, they weren't very close—there'd been some kind of falling out. I'm not certain, but I believe that Audrey may have been involved with Michael, Lucinda's ex-husband, before Lucinda and he got together. I got the impression that there's bad blood there."

"Anyone else you can think of, Donna?"

"No one else by name, but a few days before Lucinda

was murdered, an ugly old woman came charging into reception. She was ranting and raving, and demanded to see Lucinda, but reception wouldn't let her through. In the end, they had to call security to escort her out of the building. It may be nothing. I don't know."

"I don't suppose you have the woman on CCTV, do you?"

"I'm sure we will have. If you come back to the studio with me, I can show you."

Donna signed me into the studios, and took me to the security office. Moments later, I was watching the CCTV coverage of the incident, which showed an old woman walk into reception, and begin to remonstrate with the receptionist.

"Just look at her," Donna said. "She looks crazy, doesn't she?"

"She certainly does." What I didn't tell her was that I recognised that old woman.

After I'd left Donna, I made my way straight over to Ever A Wool Moment where Grandma was hard at work behind the counter, for a change. I waited until the queue had cleared, and was just about to speak, but Grandma got in first.

"Where is Kathy?"

"I told you. She's a suspect in the Lucinda Gray murder case."

"I heard on the news reports that she's been released after questioning, so why isn't she behind this counter?"

"Because, Grandma, she's upset. I think she's got more important things to worry about than working behind your counter."

"I don't employ her to sit at home on her backside. Can't you see how busy it is in here? I've been run off my feet."

"Never mind that. There's something I want to ask you."

"What is it? Hurry up, before another customer comes in."

"Why did you go to the Wool TV studios a few days ago, and threaten Lucinda Gray?"

"I didn't get the chance to threaten anyone. They wouldn't even allow me to talk to her—they threw me out. They're fortunate that I didn't turn them all into toads."

"Why were you there in the first place?"

"Because that horrible woman had run an article, on her sorry excuse for a news programme, criticising Everlasting Wool. She intimated that it was a con. I wasn't going to stand for that. I went around there to have it out with her. If she hadn't gone and got herself killed, I still would."

"Did you poison her, Grandma?"

"Of course I didn't poison her. If I wanted to get rid of the woman, I could have found a much better way of doing it, and I wouldn't have left any clues behind."

"Are you sure?"

"Yes. I'm sure. I did not kill Lucinda Gray. Anyway, forget about that. It doesn't look like you've got much on your plate at the moment. Why don't you give me a hand behind the counter?"

"Sorry, not possible. I'm busy trying to clear Kathy's name. Bye."

There were times when I could have gleefully strangled

Grandma.

***

I'd magicked myself over to Candlefield, and was standing outside Cuppy C. The place was almost deserted. Pearl was behind the cake counter; Amber was behind the tea room counter. They hadn't been exaggerating when they'd said business was slow.

Across the road, the tea room at Best Cakes looked as though it was chock-a-block. I walked over there to get a closer look. There wasn't a free seat to be had. What was going on? Why were Best Cakes doing so well when Cuppy C was almost empty?

I was just about to go back across the road when I spotted two Cuppy C regulars headed for Best Cakes. I remembered them from my time behind the counter in Cuppy C.

"Hello, there!" I called.

"Hi, Jill!" the woman said. "What are you doing over here?"

"Nothing much. Are you going to Best Cakes?"

"We are."

"If you don't mind my asking, why have you deserted Cuppy C?"

"It's their prices. We love Cuppy C, and the twins' cakes are fantastic, but they doubled the prices overnight. I don't know what they expected to happen. People don't have that kind of money."

"Doubled their prices?"

"Yeah. And from what I hear, a lot of Cuppy C customers have switched to Best Cakes. I think the twins may have to rethink their prices."

"Right, thanks. I won't keep you. See you again."

I walked back over to Cuppy C. Amber was staring into space.

"Amber!"

"Sorry, Jill. I didn't realise you were there. It's been so quiet in here that I'd almost dozed off."

"So I see. Have you seen how busy it is across the road?"

"Don't rub it in." She sighed. "All of our customers seem to have deserted us for Best Cakes. I just don't know why."

"Surely it's obvious."

"Not to me or Pearl. We've been racking our brains."

"It's because you've doubled your prices."

"Done what? We haven't changed our prices in ages. Look!" She pointed to the display of cakes. The prices were all the same as when I'd been working there. Same with the drinks.

"I don't understand. I've just seen some of your regulars across the road, and they said that they'd stopped coming here because your prices had doubled."

"There must be some kind of misunderstanding."

It might have been a misunderstanding, but I was beginning to smell a rat.

Chapter 10

When I got back to the office, Jules still looked miserable.

"Hey, Jules, cheer up. It may never happen."

"I think it already has."

"Still having problems with Jethro?"

"Yeah. He's determined to go ahead with this dance troupe thing. I told him that I didn't like the idea of him flaunting his body in front of other women, but he said that it's good money, and he enjoys the dancing. Just look at this." She held up a flyer for Jethro's new dance troupe: 'Adrenaline Boys.'

"'Adrenaline Boys'? Isn't that a bit like calling yourselves 'Sweaty Boys'?"

"I told him the name was stupid, but he said he didn't choose it. It's an existing troupe who have just lost one of their dancers. His first show is this weekend, and I'm not very happy about it." She opened a drawer, pulled out a knitting needle, and began to stab the flyer. It was like the scene from Psycho.

"Be careful! Don't stab yourself."

"This is what I think of his stupid dance troupe."

Remind me never to cross Jules.

When I walked into my office, I found Winky sitting on the sofa with another cat.

"Hello, there." The other cat addressed me. "I assume you are Jill Gooder. I'm Horatio Finemark. I'm here to provide your colleague, Mr Winky, with elocution lessons."

Winky looked thoroughly miserable.

"I see. Well I'm sorry to interrupt your lesson, but I do

need to do some work. How long will it be before you're done?"

"'*Before you're done*'," he mocked. "Oh, dear. It sounds as though you could do with elocution lessons yourself, young lady. Whatever must your clients think when you speak to them like that?"

"Hold on. I speak just fine, thank you very much. I don't need lessons on how to speak from a cat."

"I think it might be better if we continued this lesson another time," Horatio Finemark said to Winky. "When there are fewer distractions. Don't you agree?"

"Whatever." Winky shrugged.

Horatio Finemark made his way out of the window.

"He's a bit much, isn't he?" I said, after he'd gone.

"Tell me about it. He's been driving me crazy. I'll never be able to speak like that."

"I take it Bella organised the elocution lessons?"

"What do you think? Between you and me, I'm getting a bit cheesed off with the whole thing."

"Have you tried telling Bella?"

"I have, but it's fallen on deaf ears."

***

I'd tried to get in touch with Michael Gray, Lucinda Gray's ex-husband, but he wouldn't take my calls, so I decided to pay him a visit at his place of work. Gemini Chemicals was on the Speedlink industrial estate. The woman on reception called him, but he said he couldn't see me. I was getting nowhere fast, so had no option but to resort to magic.

My first problem was how to identify Michael Gray; I

had no idea what he looked like. Once I was invisible, I made my way back to reception, where I noticed a large framed photograph on the wall. It had been taken ten years earlier when Gemini Chemicals had first opened for business. The company had obviously been a much smaller concern back then because there were only ten people in the photo. Fortunately, the names of the individuals were printed below the photo. Michael Gray was third from the left. He had black hair with a side parting. At least now, I had some idea who I was looking for.

I bypassed reception with ease. It was now just a matter of finding the man himself. There were a series of laboratories, each of which had a small window in the door. The first two were empty. Inside the next, there were two women working at a bench. At the next room, I struck gold. The man was obviously older than in the photograph, but he still had exactly the same hairstyle. He was wearing goggles and a white smock, and appeared to be alone in the room.

I reversed the 'invisible' spell, opened the door and walked in.

"Mr Michael Gray?"

"What are you doing in here? Who let you in?"

"I've tried to contact you several times by phone. I'm investigating the murder of your ex-wife."

"Are you the police?"

"No. I'm a private investigator."

"Then I have nothing to say to you. Get out, or I'll call security." He reached for the phone.

"I wouldn't do that, Mr Gray."

"Why? How are you going to stop me?"

"I'm actually a witch, and have magical powers. If you pick up that phone, I'll be forced to turn you into a cockroach."

"A witch? Very funny." He picked up the receiver.

"I'm deadly serious. Watch that!" I pointed to an empty test tube which was lying on the bench beside him.

"What about it?"

"Just watch."

I cast an 'enchantment' spell, and immediately the test tube sprouted two legs and two arms, and began to walk slowly along the bench towards him. He dropped the receiver onto the cradle, and began to back away. He looked terrified.

"How did you do that?"

"Like I said—I'm a witch. Need more proof?" I slowly levitated until I was about two feet off the ground.

"That's not possible! Tell me how you did it!"

I lowered myself back to the ground. "How many times do I have to tell you? I'm a witch, and if you don't answer my questions, I *will* turn you into a cockroach. Is that what you want?"

"No! Okay, I believe you. What do you want to know?"

"How did you and Lucinda meet?"

"Through a mutual friend, at a dinner party. She was an intern at a local TV station at the time. She was ten years younger than me, but we hit it off straight away. I asked her out on a date, and it kind of went from there."

"How would you describe your marriage?"

"It was great for the first few years; we barely had a cross word. But then, things started to go wrong."

"Why was that?"

"It all started when Lucinda was promoted to news

anchor on Wool TV. It was as though I'd suddenly become an embarrassment to her. My job isn't glamorous, as you can see. I eventually found out that she was having an affair with one of the studio managers. I don't think he was the first. In the end, we drifted apart, and eventually split up. I gave that woman everything, and she treated me like dirt."

"You still sound rather bitter."

"Of course I'm bitter. I loved her. How would you feel if someone treated you so badly?"

"I heard that you'd also dated Lucinda's sister at one time."

"I did, but that was before I met Lucinda. Audrey and I went out for about six months, but it was never really serious. When I met Lucinda at the dinner party, I had no idea that she was Audrey's sister. It was only several weeks later that it came out. It was a bit embarrassing at the time, but a simple coincidence. Nothing more."

"Do you have any idea who might have wanted to kill Lucinda?"

"She had a habit of rubbing people up the wrong way. She wasn't the most tactful person in the world, and certainly not the most empathetic. But I can't think of anyone who would do something like this."

"What were you doing on the evening that Lucinda was murdered?"

"I was at home. I saw it happen live on TV."

"You watch Wool TV?"

"Not really, but I do occasionally tune in to see Lucinda."

"I thought you hated the woman?"

"I can't explain it. Every time I saw her, I just wanted to

throw something at the TV."

"Is there anyone who can vouch for the fact that you were at home that night?"

"No. I was by myself."

"Okay. Well, thank you for your time, Mr Gray."

"How long have you been a witch?"

"Before I answer that question, there's something I need to do."

I cast the 'forget' spell, made myself invisible, and left the way I'd come. When he came around, he wouldn't remember my ever being there.

Michael Gray had come across as a bitter man. Was he angry enough to kill his ex-wife? I didn't think so. He did have ready access to poisons though, so he was still in the frame.

***

When I got home that evening, Mrs Rollo was looking through her front window. As soon as I stepped out of the car, she called me over.

"Jill, do you have a minute?"

"Yes, of course. Is your grandson still here?"

"No, he's back home with his mum."

How disappointing.

"He is a little darling, isn't he?" She glowed with obvious pride. "The reason I called you over, is that I've baked a cake for the Washbridge Annual Baking Competition. Would you like to see it?"

Like I had a choice.

"Okay. Sure."

It was getting more and more difficult to pretend that

Mrs Rollo's creations were anything other than awful, and I doubted this latest one would be any better.

"Come on through." She led the way into the kitchen. "What do you think?"

She pointed to what I could only assume was supposed to be a cake. It wasn't exactly round, and it wasn't exactly square. In fact, the shape wasn't one I'd ever seen before. It looked as though it had been taken into space, and then dropped to earth.

"It's very nice, Mrs Rollo."

What? What did you expect me to say? I'm not totally heartless.

"I'm entering it in the fruit cake category."

"You're still planning on going ahead with the competition, then?"

"I wouldn't normally have dreamed of entering, but Sheila was so adamant that I should, I don't see how I can disappoint her."

"Don't you think competitions can be rather vulgar, though? Surely, just producing the cake is satisfaction enough?"

"Normally, I'd agree with you, but I've made a promise to Sheila."

"Okay. Well, good luck." She was certainly going to need it.

"Just a minute, Jill. I want to ask you a big favour."

"What's that?"

"All the competition entries have to be at Washbridge Town Hall by nine-thirty tomorrow morning."

"Right?"

"The problem is, I can't drive. I suppose I could take it on the bus, but I'm afraid I might drop it. And I don't trust taxi drivers—not since the toaster incident."

"Toaster?"

"It's a long story. Remind me to tell you about it one day. I just wondered if there was any chance you could drop it in at the Town Hall for me?"

"Of course. I'd be glad to."

"Thanks ever so much, Jill. You're a lifesaver."

"I'll pop around in the morning for it then, shall I?"

"Yes. It'll be ready. If you could just make sure to get it there before nine-thirty."

"No problem."

"You'll need to be very careful with it. I would hate for it to get spoiled en route."

Was that even possible?

"Your cake will be safe with me, Mrs Rollo."

As I made my way back to my house, Megan came out of her door.

"Hi, Jill." She was obviously dying to tell me something.

"You look very pleased with yourself."

"I am. You'll never guess what's happened."

"You got rid of your mole?"

"Yes, he's gone, but that's not my good news. I've got my first five clients."

"Already?"

"Yeah. I can't believe it. People just came flocking to see the van wherever I went."

"When you say people, were they mainly men?"

"Yeah. How did you know?"

"Just a wild guess. Anyway, congratulations."

Chapter 11

The next morning when I stepped out of the door, I spotted Blake and Jen together outside their house. They appeared to be laughing. That was a good sign after the events of the last few days. Jen caught my eye and waved. I waved back. Blake gave her a big kiss, and then she climbed into her car and drove away. When she was out of sight, Blake walked over to me.

"You two look happy this morning."

"I can't tell you what a relief it is. I've hated all this friction between us."

"So, what happened?"

"I managed to convince her that I really am a wizard."

"How did you manage that?"

"It was remarkably easy. It only took a couple of spells. After I'd made myself invisible, and shrunk myself, she had no choice but to believe me. There isn't a magician in the human world who can do that."

"She must have been shocked, though."

"She was, but she slowly came around to the idea."

"Did she have lots of questions?"

"Yeah. Most of which I couldn't answer. She wanted to know how come I was a wizard. How was I supposed to answer that? I told her that my father was a wizard and my mother was a witch."

"Did you mention Candlefield?"

"I had to, but I explained that humans aren't able to go there. I also told her that she mustn't tell anyone, under any circumstances, because there were people in Candlefield called Rogue Retrievers who would come and take me back there, and she'd never see me again."

"How did she react to that?"

"By then, she was convinced I was telling the truth, so she promised that she wouldn't tell anyone. I made sure she understood that '*anyone*' must mean '*anyone*.' Not her friends. Not her relatives. No one! She seemed relieved that she finally knew what I'd been keeping from her."

"Did you mention me?"

"No, of course not. She did ask if there were other wizards and witches living in the human world. I said there weren't many, and that it was very rare for sups to come over here. She seemed to accept that. Anyway, I'd better go, Jill, or I'll be late for work. I just thought I'd keep you posted."

"Thanks, Blake. I'm pleased it's all worked out for you. Catch you later."

As I watched him leave, I couldn't help but wonder whether I should do the same thing, and come clean with Jack. I was a little jealous of Blake. He'd lifted that terrible burden from his shoulders, and no longer had to hide the truth from his partner. That had to be a fantastic feeling. I constantly felt guilty that I couldn't tell Jack who I really was. But, I simply couldn't run the risk of being taken back to Candlefield, and not being able to see Jack, Kathy, Peter and the kids ever again.

I knocked on Mrs Rollo's door.

"Ah, Jill, you remembered. Thanks ever so much. I really do appreciate this."

"No problem, Mrs Rollo. You said the town hall, I think?"

"That's right. You'll need to use the back entrance. There should be signs to tell you where to go."

"Do I have to tell them it's your cake?"

"Just give them this sheet of paper, dear. It's my entry form. All the details are on there."

She'd put the cake, or at least what passed for a cake, into a white box.

"I thought I'd let you have one last look at it before I closed the lid."

"Hmm. It's very err—nice."

The 'thing' looked just as bad as it had the previous night. It had zero chance of winning any competition anywhere, ever, but of course, I couldn't tell Mrs Rollo that.

I carried the box carefully out to my car. I'm not sure why I was worried about dropping it because even if I'd kicked it all around the neighbourhood, it couldn't have looked any worse than it already did.

I drove to the town hall, parked around the back, and followed the signs to a small entrance. I walked in behind an elderly woman who was carrying an identical white box.

"Are you entering the competition, too?" she said.

"No. I've just brought this cake in for a neighbour."

"What category is it in?"

"Fruit cake."

"You might as well take it back home with you, then. I've won the fruit cake category for the last two years. This year will be my hat trick."

"Don't you think you might be counting your chickens before they've hatched?"

"It's a foregone conclusion. There is no one in Washbridge who can make fruitcakes like Petunia Smallpiece."

"That would be you, I take it?"

"None other. The best your friend can hope for is second place. A very distant second place."

"I guess we'll just have to see about that."

What an arrogant woman.

Now, call me a big softy, but I simply couldn't allow Mrs Rollo to become a laughing stock, so I quickly cast a spell to make sure that didn't happen.

After I'd handed over the cake and the entry form, I went back to the car. Only then did I notice that I was running low on petrol. I might have made it to the office, but I didn't want to take the risk, so I called into the next petrol station en route. After filling up with unleaded, I went inside to pay.

"Morning, Jill."

Behind the counter was Daze. Sitting next to her was Blaze.

"Hello, you two. This is your latest job, I take it?"

"Yes. It's nice to be working inside for a change," Daze said.

"And we get free coffee, too." Blaze grinned.

"We do not get free coffee, Blaze." Daze turned on him. "I've already told you that you should be paying for that."

"No one is going to know if we use these tokens."

"I'll know."

"How are things with you and Haze, Daze?" I asked.

"Okay, thanks. He's promised to take me on holiday next month. I'll be leaving Blaze in charge."

"I can't wait." Blaze grinned again.

Daze gave him a look.

"I didn't mean I couldn't wait for you to go away." Blaze shrank under her gaze. "I meant I was looking forward to having the responsibility of being in charge while you're away."

"Are you still seeing Maze, Blaze?"

"I think so."

"You don't sound very sure."

"Raze has been hanging around her, recently."

"Raze? Who's that?"

"His name is Bobby Razor, but everyone calls him Raze."

"To avoid confusion?"

"Sorry?"

"Never mind. You were saying?"

"Raze is another Rogue Retriever. He fancies himself as a bit of a lady's man. If I catch him with Maze, I'll stick one on him."

"How is the Rogue Retriever business doing anyway?"

"We've been really busy," Daze said.

"You can say that again," Blaze agreed. "The last few days have been murder."

"It's the fallout from the closure of Bar Scarlet." Daze handed back my credit card. "We've been rounding up the remaining rogue vampires over the last few days. I think we've caught them all now, so hopefully, we can have a bit of a breather."

"Why are you over here at the moment?"

"It's a full moon," Daze said. "Need I say more?"

"Ah, right. Expecting werewolf trouble?"

"It's the same every month. There's always a handful who can't control themselves. As you probably already know, the majority go back to the werewolf Range in Candlefield, and let loose in there. It's the safest option. A few stay here and play it safe by isolating themselves in the countryside where they can't do any harm to anyone. But there are a few who can't resist trying to scare humans. They're more of an annoyance than anything else. And then there are those who take it too far, and actually attack humans. They're the ones we're after. We're going to mount a patrol around Washbridge Park tonight. That's one of their favourite haunts."

While I was there I decided to pick Daze's brain.

"Daze, could I have a quick word in private?"

"Sure. Blaze, can you watch the till?"

He swapped seats with her, and Daze followed me to the other end of the shop.

"There's a couple of things I wanted to talk to you about. First off, I wanted to ask you about relationships between sups and humans. Do you find there are many cases where the sup ends up getting taken back to Candlefield?"

"A lot. It happens most weeks. The problem is that most couples think it will be easy to keep the secret, but it never is. It doesn't matter how close the couple are, there's always the danger that it will get out, and when it does, we invariably hear about it. Sometimes, the couples have been together for decades, and the human has known their partner was a sup the whole of that time. Sooner or later, it comes out, and then we have to act. We have no choice but to take the sup back. It can be heart-breaking at times." Daze hesitated. "You're not thinking of telling Jack that you're a witch, are you?"

"Me? No, I would never do that. I agree with you. It's way too dangerous. I was just curious, that's all."

"What's the other thing you wanted to talk to me about?"

"The twins told me that you attended Candlefield Academy of Supernatural Studies."

"That's right."

"I've been invited to give a talk there, and I wondered if I might pick your brain about the place?"

"Sure, but there isn't really time now. Let's meet up in Cuppy C sometime, and I'll tell you whatever you want to know then."

"That would be great. Thanks."

***

When I walked into the office, Mrs V was behind her desk. Standing next to it was Armi. He had a pot on his leg, and was on crutches.

"Oh, dear," I said.

"Oh, dear, indeed." Mrs V sighed. "So much for our dinner and dance at the Cuckoo Clock Appreciation Society."

"What happened?"

"Well, Jill." Armi managed a smile. "It's a bit embarrassing, actually."

"Stupidity, I'd call it," Mrs V said. It was obvious that she was none too pleased with him.

"I'd just left the office, and was walking down the street, when I came across a window cleaner. I'm quite superstitious, so I didn't want to walk under his ladder. I stepped to one side, but I hadn't seen the black cat. I fell over it, and broke my ankle."

How I managed to keep a straight face, I do not know.

Winky was sitting at my desk. Seated opposite him was

another cat. At first glance, I thought I'd walked in on another elocution lesson, but then I realised it wasn't Horatio Finemark.

"What's going on?"

"Social etiquette." Winky sounded beyond bored.

That's when I noticed the cutlery that had been set out on my desk. The cat sitting opposite Winky totally ignored me. "Winky, which one is the soup spoon?"

"I never eat soup." Winky yawned. "Is there a salmon spoon?"

"I don't think your heart is in this." The other cat was obviously not amused. "Perhaps we should call it a day. Give me a call if and when you do decide to take the matter seriously, would you?"

The cat jumped off the chair, ran across the room, and disappeared out of the window.

"Stuff this." Winky swiped his paw across the desk, knocking the cutlery onto the floor. "I've had enough of elocution lessons, deportment lessons, and all this etiquette nonsense. If Bella wants to go out with me, she's just going to have to take me as she finds me."

"Good for you." It was nice to see Winky back to his old self. I hated to see him kowtowing to anyone. Except me, of course—some chance of that!

He jumped down from the desk. "I think it's time for salmon."

"Red, not pink?"

"Obviously."

I'd just finished feeding Winky when my phone rang.

"Jill?" It was Sarah Travers who'd been to see me a few days earlier.

"Yes, Sarah?"

"I promised I'd call you the next time Jerry said he was going to play squash."

"You did. I take it he has?"

"Yes, out of the blue, as always. He told me this morning, just before he set off for work. I didn't get a chance to ask him any questions because he was already out of the door. Will you be able to tail him as you promised?"

"Yes. I think the easiest thing will be for me to follow him after he comes out of work. If you give me the name and address of his place of work, and a rough idea of what time he finishes, then I'll be waiting for him. I've got the photo which you sent me, so I should be able to spot him."

"That sounds great, Jill. Thanks."

It turned out that the offices where Sarah's husband worked were only a fifteen-minute walk from mine. I'd be waiting for him when he came out.

Chapter 12

"Hello?" The man sounded half asleep when he answered the phone.

"Is that Callum Hamilton?"

"Yes. Who's this?"

"My name's Jill Gooder. I'm a private investigator, working on the Lucinda Gray case."

"Oh, right. How can I help?"

"I wonder if we could meet up? I'd like to ask you a few questions."

"I can't today. I'm out of town, working on a modelling assignment."

"When will you be back?"

"Tomorrow."

"Okay. How about I call you then to arrange a time and place?"

"Yeah. That's fine."

Maybe I was being unfairly judgemental, after all it had been only a brief exchange, but the man hadn't exactly sounded distraught considering his girlfriend had been murdered only a few days earlier.

"Jill?" Mrs V popped her head around the door. "Your accountant's here."

"Mr Roberts? Again?"

"No, the other one. Mr Stone."

"Oh, right. Show him in."

Luther Stone usually had a huge smile on his face, but not today. In fact, he looked rather glum.

"Do come in, Luther. Have a seat. Is everything okay?"

"It was until I received this." He had an envelope in his

hand.

"What is it?"

"It's the letter you sent me. I just wanted to ask why you've decided to terminate our arrangement."

"I've done no such thing."

"Then I'm confused." He took the letter out of the envelope, and put it on my desk. It purported to come from me, and was short and to the point:

Dear Mr Stone,

Thank you for the accountancy services you have provided to me, but please accept this as my notice to terminate the arrangement forthwith.

Yours sincerely,

Jill Gooder.

The signature definitely wasn't mine.

"I don't know anything about this, Luther."

"So, you don't want to cancel our arrangement?"

"Certainly not."

"I've received three similar letters today from other clients. I was beginning to think I'd done something to upset everyone. You're the first person I've been to see."

"I wonder who can have done this." I didn't say so, but I was almost certain I knew who had sent the letter. How dare Robert Roberts write to Luther to tell him I wanted to terminate my contract? Surely, he couldn't have expected to get away with it? Hadn't he realised that Luther would double-check?

"By the way, Luther, did you know that Betty has opened a shop on the high street?"

"I did. I drove past there the other day. I was quite surprised."

"She has always had an interest in seashells."

"I don't mean I was surprised by the theme of the shop; that was an obvious choice for her. No, I'm surprised that she could afford to embark upon such a venture. When she and I were together, she was living from month to month; she didn't have any savings. I can't work out where she found the money to finance the business. I can only assume she managed to persuade the bank to give her a big loan. I just hope she knows what she's doing because to the best of my knowledge, she has no retail experience. Still, I wish her the best of luck. No hard feelings, and all that. Anyway, I suppose I should get going. Hopefully, the other letters will prove to be hoaxes too. Bye, Jill, and thanks again."

When Robert Roberts had come to see me, he'd sounded determined to win back his customers, but I'd no idea that he intended to go to these lengths. If the man could do something so sly, I wasn't sure I'd ever trust him with my books.

It struck me that I hadn't seen anything of Winky for an hour or so. That wasn't like him; he liked to annoy me on a regular basis. I got up from my desk, walked over to the sofa, and knelt down, so I could see underneath it. He was reading a book.

"What's that you're reading, Winky? Another etiquette guide?"

"Nah. I'm done with all that nonsense." He held up the book.

"'Fly Fishing for Felines'?"

"Yep."

"A strange choice, isn't it?"

"Since when is it unusual for a cat to be interested in fish?" His impatience was showing.

"I know you're interested in eating fish, but catching them?"

"Why not? It cuts out the middle man."

"Where exactly would you go fishing?"

"There are plenty of places around here, if you know where to look."

"What about all the equipment you're going to need?"

"Don't worry. It's all in hand."

Knowing Winky, it probably was.

What I needed was a blueberry muffin, and not just any blueberry muffin. I needed one from Cuppy C. No one had blueberry muffins to match those sold by the twins.

I magicked myself over to Candlefield. Standing outside Cuppy C, I could see that the place was deserted yet again. If things carried on like this, the twins would be in real trouble. Flora and Laura were behind the counter, but there was no sign of the twins. They'd probably gone shopping. That's what they did when they were feeling a bit down, or whenever there was a 'Y' in the name of the day.

The twins had denied ever raising their prices, and yet when I'd spoken to a couple of their ex-regulars, they'd insisted that the reason they'd deserted Cuppy C was because of the price increase. Something weird was going on.

Flora and Laura hadn't seen me, so I cast a spell to disguise myself as an old woman, and then made my way inside the shop.

"Yes, dear?" Laura said.

"A cup of tea and one of your delicious blueberry muffins, please." What a character actor I was—Hollywood was calling.

"Certainly. Coming up."

The prices of the cakes and buns were all double what they should have been. I glanced at the drinks price list. They too had doubled. Laura handed me the tea and a muffin, and then took my money.

This explained a lot.

I took a seat next to the window. The muffin was delicious, but it wasn't worth twice the normal price. No wonder the customers had been deserting Cuppy C in droves. The two ice maidens, Flora and Laura, must have waited until the twins were out, and then used magic to increase the price of everything. That would also explain why, before the customers started going elsewhere, the takings had been up on the days when the ice maidens had been left in charge. This was sabotage. There was no other word for it.

Some time back, I'd seen Flora and Laura talking to Miles Best, and I couldn't help but wonder if he was behind all of this. I considered confronting them there and then, but thought better of it. It wasn't my shop, so I shouldn't be the one to do it. That was for the twins to do. I had to let them know what the two evil ice maidens had been up to.

***

Back in Washbridge, I arrived at Diamond Ceramics ten minutes before Sarah Travers' husband, Jerry, was due to leave. I knew what he looked like from the photograph she'd emailed to me. I'd never liked working on infidelity cases. There was no sense of achievement when I caught someone cheating. There were no happy endings for anyone involved. But, they paid the bills, and someone had to do it.

I was beginning to think that he wasn't going to show. The staff had been coming out for fifteen minutes, but there was still no sign of Jerry Travers. Then he appeared. I was on the opposite side of the road, and deliberately kept my distance. He had a sports bag with him, so maybe he was going to play squash, after all. Was it possible that he now played at a different club? Sarah didn't think so, and besides, he'd told her that he was still going to the same club. The one which Sarah now knew had closed its squash courts.

He went into a restaurant called The Ponds. If he had arranged to meet another woman, I'd have the thankless task of having to tell his wife. Fortunately, he chose a table that was by the window, so I was able to keep an eye on him without having to follow him inside. The waitress gave him a menu, and then brought him a drink. A few minutes later, she returned to take his order. The service was painfully slow, but Jerry Travers seemed to be in no hurry. Watching him eat made me hungry. I'd only had a muffin, and I was absolutely starving.

Throughout the meal, he spoke to no one except for the waitress. By the time he'd finished and paid his bill, it was starting to get dark outside. I was still standing across the road. I was tired, thirsty, and hungry, but I had to stick with him to find out what he was up to. According to Sarah, on the nights when he supposedly went to play squash, her husband didn't get back home until the early hours of the morning, so there was still plenty of time for him to meet up with someone.

I followed him again, still keeping my distance. After a while, it became obvious that he was headed towards Washbridge Park. I would need to get closer to him because the lighting in the park was almost non-existent. Why would he go there after dark? It made no sense.

And then, the penny dropped.

It was a full moon!

I had to catch up with him; there wasn't a moment to lose. As I ran down the hill, he disappeared into a clump of bushes. Moments later, I charged through those same bushes, and eventually came upon a small clearing. Jerry Travers was standing there; he was just about to take his shirt off.

As soon as I got close to him, my senses confirmed my suspicions. He was a werewolf. I cursed myself for being so stupid. If I'd got closer to him earlier, I would have sensed it immediately, but I'd deliberately kept my distance so that he wouldn't spot me.

He spun around. "Who are you?"

"Your wife asked me to follow you."

"Oh, no." He looked shocked. "I knew this would happen one day. Does she know?"

"That you're a werewolf? No. She thinks you're cheating on her."

"What? Why would she think that?"

"What did you expect? The squash courts where you're supposed to be playing tonight have been closed for months."

"I had no idea."

"Your wife knows you've been lying to her. She's known for a long time. That's why she hired me to follow you."

"But you're a witch."

"I'm also a private investigator. It's a good thing for you that I'm a sup. If she'd gone to any other P.I, you'd really be in trouble. What do you think would have happened if a human had found you just now?"

"I dread to think."

"You can't go werewolf here."

"I have to. Any moment now, I'll change anyway. I can't stop it."

"The Rogue Retrievers are patrolling this park tonight."

"How do you know?"

"I just do. If you go werewolf in here tonight, you'll be back in Candlefield before the morning."

"What am I going to do? I'm going to change any moment now."

"Grab your bag, and take my hand."

He did as I said, and I magicked us both over to the werewolf Range in Candlefield.

"Get in there. And from now on, you come here every month. Understand?"

"Yes, of course. But what about Sarah?"

"Don't worry about that. I have an idea."

I told him my plan, and he agreed to go along with it. I then magicked myself back to Washbridge and made a call.

"Sarah?"

"Jill? Have you found him? Is he seeing someone else?"

"No, he isn't."

"What is he doing? Where has he been going?"

"You're not going to like this. He's been playing poker with his friends into the early hours of the morning. He told me that you are totally against gambling."

"I am, but I'd rather he was doing that than having an affair. I just wish he'd told me."

"The two of you will need to have a long talk. Maybe you could see your way clear to allowing him to play once a month?"

"I suppose so—provided it doesn't go beyond that."

"I'm sure it won't. Once a month will be absolutely fine."

Chapter 13

"Grandma! Wait for me. Grandma!"

She was ahead of me in the corridor, but no matter how fast I ran, I couldn't catch up with her.

"Grandma! Stop!"

She didn't seem to hear me.

There were no doors on either side of the corridor, which turned first this way, and then that.

"Grandma! Stop!"

Eventually, she came to a staircase, and began to descend. I followed. When I reached the bottom, I found her standing in front of a door. There was danger behind it; something evil was lurking in there.

"Grandma! Don't open that door!"

She turned around. "Jill? What are you doing here?"

"Don't open that door, Grandma. It's dangerous."

"Don't be silly. It's perfectly safe." She turned the handle.

I sat up in bed, in a cold sweat.

Not again! I'd had that same horrible nightmare, but this time, I'd been following Grandma instead of Aunt Lucy. She'd ended up at the same door, and despite my warning that there was danger lurking inside, she'd opened it. But what was in there? Once again, I'd woken before I could find out.

The horrible images from the nightmare were still buzzing around my head as I showered and dressed. I had no appetite for breakfast, and managed just a few mouthfuls of corn flakes.

I'd no sooner stepped out of the door than I heard Mrs

Rollo calling to me. She came rushing over; I'd never seen her move so fast.

"Jill. Wait!" She was positively beaming.

"Mrs Rollo. Slow down. You'll hurt yourself."

"I've got great news."

Only then did I notice that she had something in her hand.

"Look." She held up the tiniest trophy I'd ever seen. It was barely three inches high.

"Look what I've won! It's for the best fruit cake. I'm so proud. I didn't think I stood a chance, but I won first prize."

Engraved on the front of the trophy was: 'First Prize. Fruit Cake Category. Mrs Rita Rollo.'

"That's great."

I didn't have the heart to tell her that the only reason she'd won was because I'd replaced her monstrosity with a cake I'd magicked up for the occasion. So much for Petunia Smallpiece's hat trick.

***

I'd arranged to meet Callum Hamilton at Washbridge Studios where he was scheduled to do a photo shoot. It took me a while to find the place; the only sign was a small plaque next to the door. I pressed the buzzer, but no one responded. I waited a few seconds and tried again. This time, the door clicked open, and I stepped inside.

"Are you Callum?"

The guy was bald, and in his forties. He certainly wasn't how I'd pictured Callum Hamilton.

"No, I'm Shane Fairweather. This is my studio. Who are

you?"

There was something familiar about the man. I felt as though I knew him from somewhere, but I couldn't think where.

"My name's Jill Gooder. I'm a private investigator. I arranged to meet Callum Hamilton here today."

"That's just dandy! So not only is he going to turn up late as per usual, but he expects me to hang around while he talks to you. Well, he's got another think coming. I'm sorry, lady, but assuming he does ever turn up, you'll have to wait in line. I need to get this session rolling."

"That's fine. I don't want to interfere with your work. Is he often late?"

"Always, but then they're all the same. Appointments and deadlines seem to mean nothing to them these days. What do you want to speak to him about, anyway?"

"The recent death at Wool TV."

"Lucinda Gray?"

"That's right. Did you know her?"

"Callum has mentioned her name. I believe he's been seeing her. You'd better take a seat over there in the corner. And please don't distract Callum while he's working."

Callum eventually turned up thirty minutes later.

"What time do you call this?" Shane Fairweather was none too pleased.

"Sorry, mate. I got delayed. You know how it is."

"Not really. I always manage to get here on time."

Callum Hamilton was tall and slim. With his bed hair, he looked as though he'd just been dragged through a hedge backwards.

"You'd better go and see Jean," Fairweather said.

"Hurry up."

I guessed that Jean must be the makeup artist. Callum certainly needed one.

Fifteen minutes later, he re-emerged; the transformation was incredible. He had gone from slob to eye candy. His hair was now immaculate, and he looked every bit the model.

"Hurry up." Fairweather's patience was growing thin. "Start with the blue cardigan, would you?"

Callum had been booked to model a range of knitwear for an Autumn collection. He may not have been a good timekeeper, but once in front of the lens, he became the consummate professional, following Fairweather's instructions to the letter. An hour later, and the photo shoot was finished. Shane Fairweather began to pack up his equipment, and Callum made his way over to me.

"Sorry to keep you waiting."

"No problem."

"I had planned to get here earlier, but you know how it is. It can be difficult to get out of bed some mornings."

"I understand."

"How come you're investigating Lucinda's murder? Who hired you to do it?"

"No one hired me as such. My sister, Kathy, works at Wool TV."

"Oh, yeah. I know her. She does the weekly magazine show, doesn't she?"

"That's right. The police are treating her as a suspect."

"Really? I can't believe she had anything to do with it."

"She didn't. That's why I'm trying to find out who did. Could you tell me how you and Lucinda met?"

"I do a lot of work at Wool TV, modelling their

knitwear. The two of us got chatting one day, and we seemed to hit it off."

"Was she still married to Michael when you started seeing each other?"

"No. That was long since over. She'd been out with a few other guys since then. We hadn't been seeing each other very long at all. Only a few weeks, in fact."

"When did you last see her?"

"The same day she died. She came to see me here, as it happens. We'd arranged to meet at about ten am, but I was late." He smiled. "I'm often late. When I got here, she was arguing with Shane, but you've seen how he is. He hates people interrupting his shoots."

"I heard that you had a somewhat fiery relationship with Lucinda?"

"Who told you that?"

"I'd rather not say. Is it true?"

"I wouldn't call it fiery. I'd call it passionate."

"Is there anyone you can think of who might have wanted to hurt Lucinda?"

"She could be a bit abrasive, and often rubbed people up the wrong way. Not enough to make someone want to kill her though."

"Had she received any threats?"

"If she had, she never mentioned them to me."

"So she didn't seem worried about anything? She wasn't acting differently?"

"No, nothing like that."

"Where were you on the evening that Lucinda was murdered?"

"In my flat. I'd done three photo shoots that day, and I was absolutely spent. I bought a bottle of wine, and was waiting for Lucinda to come over."

"Can anyone vouch for that?"

"No. I was by myself all evening."

Just like Michael Gray, Callum had supposedly been alone that evening. It may have been true, but it was also very convenient. It still bothered me that Callum didn't seem at all affected by Lucinda's untimely death, but then they had only been seeing one another for a few weeks.

***

I'd arranged to meet the twins at Aunt Lucy's.

"What's this all about, Jill?" Amber said.

"Yeah, why have you dragged us here?" Pearl complained.

"I wanted to talk to you away from the shop. Away from any eavesdroppers."

"About what?" Amber said.

"I think I might know why Cuppy C is losing customers."

Now I had their attention.

"I'm absolutely sure that Flora and Laura are behind it."

"Oh, give it a rest, Jill." Amber sighed.

"What is it with you and the girls?" Pearl said. "Why have you got it in for them? Flora and Laura are okay. I don't know why you don't like them."

"They've got you both fooled."

"No they haven't," Pearl objected. "We're not stupid."

"Just hear me out. The other day, when you'd left them in charge of the shop, I went in there in disguise. They thought they were serving a little old lady."

"So?"

"So, they had doubled all the prices."

"Are you sure?"

"I'm positive. Every price was twice what it should have been."

"I'll kill them!" Pearl said. "I'm going to go back there now, and kill them."

"Hold on." I grabbed her arm. "We need to catch them in the act."

"How are we meant to do that?" Amber said.

"We'll all go there in disguise, just like I did the other day."

"That's not going to work," Pearl said. "Our magic isn't strong enough to fool them. They'll see straight through it."

"Not if I cast the spell on all three of us. When they look at us, they'll see three old ladies. That way you'll be able to see the prices for yourselves."

The twins agreed, so I cast the spell. The three of us now looked like old biddies.

"Look at you." Amber pointed at Pearl. "You're really old, and ugly. You look like Grandma."

"You can't talk." Pearl laughed. "You make Grandma look attractive."

It took us a while to walk over there; we had to stay in character. When we got to Cuppy C, Flora recognised 'old lady' me.

"Hello, dear. Back again? Same as last time, is it? A cup of tea and a blueberry muffin? What about your two friends?"

The twins were staring wide-eyed at the prices, all of which had been doubled. That was my cue. I reversed the spell, and the three of us reverted to our normal appearance. Flora and Laura looked gobsmacked.

"You two are sacked!" Pearl spat the words.

"And you can get out of your rooms right now!" Amber said. "How dare you do this to us? You could have put us out of business."

It didn't take Flora and Laura long to recover their composure.

"You two were easy to fool." Laura grinned. "You're idiots."

"Get out of here," Pearl yelled.

I had to hold her back, otherwise she would have been over the counter to them.

"It'll be our pleasure to get out of this dump," Laura said. "But don't think you've heard the last of us. Cuppy C's days are numbered."

They both cackled as they disappeared upstairs. The twins were still seething, so it was left to me to cast a spell to change the prices back to what they should have been.

"We're going to have to do some advertising," Pearl said. "To let people know that our prices are back to normal. We'll place an advert in The Candle."

"Thanks, Jill," Amber said. "You may just have saved Cuppy C."

"Yeah. Thanks, Jill. I'm sorry we doubted you."

"That's okay. I'm just pleased everything turned out all right."

Moments later, the two ice maidens came downstairs, carrying their suitcases.

"Get out," Pearl shouted. "Get out of here now!"

"Our pleasure," Flora said.

"We'll be seeing you soon." Laura gave us a little wave.

Chapter 14

It had just turned midday when I arrived at the office. Jules was busy knitting.

"Have you managed to sort things out with Jethro?"

"No. He still insists that he's going to resume his dancing career."

"What are you going to do?"

"I don't know. I really like him, but I'm not sure I can handle the idea of him strutting his stuff in front of a room full of women."

"Time to give him an ultimatum, maybe?"

I'd just started towards my office door when Jules called after me, "By the way, Jill, don't forget that it's Woolcon on Friday."

I'd been hoping I might worm my way out of that, but Jules and Mrs V were never going to let me. Whatever had possessed me to agree to go to a convention where adults walked around dressed as knitting needles or balls of wool? One thing was for sure—Jill Gooder wouldn't be wearing a silly costume—I was way too sensible to participate in anything so puerile. I'd told Mrs V and Jules in no uncertain terms that I wasn't getting dressed up.

Thirty minutes later, Grandma came charging into my office. She was obviously not best pleased about something; the wart on the end of her nose was glowing red again.

"Do you have an appointment?" I quipped.

What? I'm not scared of Grandma. Well, not much, anyway.

"I don't need an appointment to see my granddaughter. They're still at it!"

"Who is still at what?"

"Those fish people. They're still blocking my window! I thought you were going to do something about it."

"I did have a word with them. I'm sure that promotion won't go on for much longer."

"It's gone on too long already. If you can't stop them, then I guess I'll just turn them into toads."

"You can't do that, Grandma."

"Who says?"

"I do."

"And since when did you give me orders, young lady?"

"It's not an order. It's a request from your granddaughter. Please don't turn them into toads."

"Okay. I won't turn them into toads."

"Do you promise?"

"Yes, I promise." She stormed back out of the office.

I wasn't sure if I should believe her or not, but I hoped for Betty's sake that Grandma would keep her word.

An hour later, my phone rang. It was Betty Longbottom; she sounded desperate.

"Jill! You've got to help me!"

"Whatever's the matter?"

"Can you come down here now, please?"

Before I could ask any more questions, the line went dead. Even though I didn't consider Betty to be one of my best friends, I couldn't ignore her plea for help.

When I arrived at She Sells, Betty was waiting for me by the door.

"Jill, come in."

As I did, she turned the sign on the door to read 'closed.'

"What is it, Betty? What's wrong?"

"Come through to the back, and you'll see for yourself."

I followed her into what appeared to be a large store room. Lying on the floor were the three giant sea creatures. The people inside the costumes were desperately trying to get out of them, but without any success.

"Something's happened to these costumes!" Betty screamed at me. "They've been trying to get out of them for the last thirty minutes, but the costumes are getting smaller all the time. Your grandmother must have done this."

"How can she have made them shrink? That doesn't make any sense."

"I don't know, but how else could it have happened?"

I knew that Betty was right. Grandma was definitely behind this. As always, she had been very smart. She'd promised that she wouldn't turn them into toads, but she hadn't said that there wouldn't be some other kind of reprisal. And this was no doubt it. Even as I was standing there, I could see that the costumes were slowly getting smaller and smaller. I had to do something quickly, or I didn't like to think what might happen to the poor people trapped inside them. But, I couldn't do anything while Betty was watching. I had to get her out of there.

"Betty! Go and find some scissors!"

"What good will they do? They'll never cut through those costumes."

"Don't argue! Just go and get them!"

Betty looked doubtful, but did as I asked, and disappeared into the shop. As soon as she'd gone, I concocted a spell which would make the costumes grow larger. It was my only option because I wasn't sure how to reverse Grandma's original spell.

As soon as the costumes were back to their normal size, the two women and one man, who had been trapped inside, managed to clamber out. Moments later, Betty came rushing back into the room with a pair of scissors in her hand.

"How did they get out?" She stared in disbelief.

"Beats me." I shrugged.

The two women and the man hurried out of the shop. I doubted that they'd be back the next day.

"I don't know what you did, Jill, but thanks," Betty said. "I owe you one."

"Forget it." I started for the door, but then noticed a glass jar on top of the cupboard. Inside it were hundreds of bottle tops.

Betty must have followed my gaze because she took my arm, and tried to lead me out. "Come on, Jill. I'll see you out."

"Just a minute. What's in the jar?"

"What jar?"

I pulled my arm free, and made my way across the room.

"This jar!" I picked it up and shook it. "Are these Norman's bottle tops?"

"Of course not. They're mine."

"You're lying, Betty. You've never collected bottle tops."

"I've just started."

"In that case, you won't mind if I show these to Norman, will you?"

"Okay, okay. They are Norman's."

"How could you steal from your ex-boyfriend?"

"I needed the money. I'd run out of funds. Opening this shop has cost much more than I'd expected."

"So you thought you'd help yourself to Norman's bottle tops?"

"I'm sorry." Betty took a seat. She was close to tears. "What are you going to do, Jill?"

"What do you think? I'm going to tell Norman."

"Please don't, Jill. I'll do anything!"

***

I wasn't sure what to do about Betty and the bottle tops, so I decided to sleep on it. Jack wasn't due back until the next day, so I called at Kathy's on the way home.

"Jill?" Kathy came to the door wearing a T-shirt and jogging bottoms. "Is there any news?"

"On the Lucinda case? Sorry, no. I just came over to see how you were doing."

"You'd better come in. Do you want a coffee?"

"I'll make it. Come through to the kitchen with me, and we can talk."

"Who have you spoken to so far?" Kathy asked.

"Donna Proudlove, Michael Gray and Callum Hamilton. But to be honest with you, I'm no further forward. Have you heard anything from Wool TV?"

"They've suspended all live programmes for this week. They're showing a series of reruns, and hoping to return to normal programming next week. I'm not sure I'll be ready to return by then unless this lot is all sorted out."

"Where are the kids?"

"Mikey stayed behind at school for football practice.

Peter will pick him up afterwards. Lizzie is at Jodie's house—she's one of her friends from school. I'm hoping Lizzie will be a bit happier when she gets back than she was this morning."

"Why? What's the matter?"

"Can you remember that bear of hers? The one that she said was her new best friend?"

"Joe Bear?"

"Wow! I'm impressed you remember his name."

"What's wrong with Joe Bear?"

"He's disappeared."

"Disappeared how?"

"I've no idea. Lizzie says she brought him back from school yesterday, but that he went missing overnight. I don't see how he could have—I think she must have left him at school. Hopefully, she'll have found him there today."

It looked like my 'enchantment' spell hadn't worked as well as I thought it had. Joe Bear must have gone 'rogue.'

After we'd finished coffee, I made my excuses and left, with the promise that I'd keep Kathy posted on any news related to the Lucinda Gray affair.

Where would an enchanted teddy bear go? I racked my brain, and could think of only one place nearby. Cosmo Toy Emporium was a grand name for a very small shop. It was less than a quarter of a mile from Kathy's house. The shop sold all manner of toys, but specialised in soft toys.

"Good afternoon, Madam," the bearded man behind the counter greeted me with a smile. He had a look of Santa Claus about him. "Are you looking for anything in particular?"

"A teddy bear. For my niece."

"In that case, you want the second aisle on the right."

As soon as I turned down that aisle, I knew I was in the right place.

"Has anyone ever told you that you have beautiful eyes?" a deep voice said. "What are you doing tonight?"

Joe Bear was standing on the second shelf, trying to chat up a pretty pink bear who had a white ribbon around her head.

"Hey, you!" I said in a whisper. "What are you doing in here?"

Joe Bear looked surprised to see me. "I was getting bored. All that little girl wants me to do is read fairy stories to her. She has no conversation whatsoever, so I thought I'd try my luck down here."

"Tough luck, buddy. You're needed elsewhere." I grabbed hold of him, and made my way to the door.

"Hold on, young lady," Santa Claus called after me. "Where do you think you're going with that bear?"

"This is my—err—that's to say—err. How much is it?"

"Fifteen pounds."

Great!

I knocked on Kathy's door.

"Jill?" She looked surprised to see me again so soon, but even more surprised to see what I had in my hand.

"I found this just down the road. Lizzie must have dropped it on her way home from school yesterday." I passed the bear to Kathy, and made a quick exit before she could ask any awkward questions.

***

When I arrived home, I was surprised and delighted to

see that Jack's car was already on the driveway. I hadn't been expecting him until the following day.

"Jack?"

"Up here." His voice came from our bedroom. "I'll be down in a minute."

I went through to the kitchen, and switched on the kettle. This warranted a custard cream celebration.

"I got away early." He grabbed me around the waist, and gave me a peck on the lips. "What's happening with Kathy? Any news?"

"They haven't charged her, but she still appears to be the prime suspect."

"I see The Bugle has linked Lucinda Gray's death with the earlier poisoning."

"Do you think there's anything in that?"

"I don't know. I guess it's possible."

"Leo Riley should be able to tell us. Why don't you try him again?"

"I'd be wasting my time, Jill. I'm persona non grata in his books. And, before you suggest it, you should steer clear of him too. Nothing good can come from getting his back up. Promise you won't go near him."

"I promise."

Liar, liar, pants on fire. I'd already decided it was time to pay Mr Leo Riley a visit, but I wasn't about to tell Jack that—I couldn't handle the aggro.

"Is there anything I can do?" he offered.

"Yes. You can give me a proper kiss."

"I can do better than that."

***

Later—much later—we were in the kitchen, washing the dishes.

"Oh, I forgot to mention," Jack said. "We've had an invitation."

"To what?"

"A wedding. It was addressed to both of us. I left it in the bedroom."

He wiped his hands, and hurried upstairs. Moments later, he came back down with a pink envelope in his hand. "Who are Deli and Nails?"

My heart sank. I'd tried to put Deli's wedding out of my mind, in the hope that she and Nails might call it off.

"Deli is my friend's mother. Nails is her boyfriend."

"What kind of name is Nails? Is he some kind of hard man? As in 'hard as nails'?"

"Something like that." I didn't want to gross Jack out by telling him the truth. "I'll make some excuse so we don't have to go."

"No! Don't do that! I love a good wedding, and I'd like to meet more of your friends. I barely know any of them."

Oh bum!

Chapter 15

It was nice to have Jack home. I couldn't imagine going back to living by myself. He was having a lie in, and he'd had the cheek to ask me to bring him breakfast in bed. I must be going soft in my old age because I did it: Tea, toast and marmalade on a tray. The next time I had a lie in, he'd better do the same for me, or there'd be trouble.

I glanced across the road at Blake's house. I hadn't heard any more from them since he'd proven to Jen that he was a wizard. Hopefully, everything was okay over there.

I was just about to get into my car when I heard a 'toot, toot.' Mr Hosey was coming down the road on his stupid little train.

"Good morning, Jill." He tooted his horn again. "And how are you this morning?"

"Fine, thanks. You're up bright and early this morning, Mr Hosey."

"I've been working on Bessie for the last few days, so I'm just taking her for a quick spin, to make sure everything is okay."

"Right. Well, I'd better get going. Lots to do."

"Before you go, Jill, I wanted to let you know that I'll be holding an open house on Tuesday, for people to come and look at my model railway. No children allowed, obviously. I'm sure you and Jack will want to come."

I would rather have chewed glass while walking on hot coals.

"We've arranged to go to see Jack's brother on Tuesday," I lied. "What a pity—maybe another time. Anyway, must go. Bye, Mr Hosey."

Another bullet dodged.

***

"Jill, thank goodness you're here." Mrs V collared me as soon as I walked through the door.

"What is it, Mrs V? Whatever's the matter?"

"It's your grandmother."

"Is she okay? Has something happened to her?"

"She's been taken in for questioning by the police."

"When?"

"Only a few minutes ago. She rang the office, and was quite annoyed that you weren't here. She said she only had the one phone call, and that I'd better get in touch with you quickly. I was just about to call you on your mobile."

"Is that all she said? That the police had taken her in for questioning?"

"Yes, she was only on the line for a couple of minutes."

"I suppose I'd better get down there. Do I have any appointments this morning?"

Mrs V gave me *that* look. Of course I didn't have any appointments.

Fortunately, the reception area at Washbridge police station was deserted. The officer behind the desk actually looked pleased to see me; he was obviously bored out of his brain.

"How can I help you, madam?"

"My grandmother has been brought in for questioning. I'd like to see her, please."

"What's her name?"

"Mirabel Millbright. I believe she's here in connection with the Lucinda Gray murder case."

"Just a moment, please. Let me go and check." He disappeared through the door behind him. A few minutes later, he reappeared. "Are you by any chance Jill Gooder?"

"Yes, I am."

"Detective Riley would like a word with you."

"Good. I'd like a word with him too. Where is he?"

"He said you should take a seat. He'll be with you, shortly."

"How long is 'shortly'?"

"Just take a seat, please, madam."

This wasn't the first time that Leo Riley had kept me waiting. I was convinced he did it on purpose. Fifty minutes later, he finally appeared.

"Where's my grandmother?"

"Come with me."

I followed him down the corridor, and into a small interview room.

"Where is she?"

"Patience, woman!"

"I asked where my grandmother is."

"All in good time."

"Have you charged her with anything?"

"No. Not yet."

"What do you mean: 'not yet'? Why did you even bring her in?"

"I think you already know the answer to that. From what I hear, you've viewed the CCTV footage from the Wool TV studio, haven't you?"

"Yes. And any idiot could see that she didn't get inside

the building."

"Not on that occasion, maybe. But who's to say that she didn't come back?"

"Don't be ridiculous. This is just harassment. First my sister, and now my grandmother. This is looking awfully like a vendetta against me."

"Don't flatter yourself. I've got better things to do than worry about you and your family. Your grandmother will be released in a few minutes."

"Are you linking Lucinda's murder with the earlier poisoning?"

"I'll tell you the same thing as I told the reporter from The Bugle. No comment."

"The Bugle seems to think they're connected."

"If The Bugle says so, then I guess they must be." He scoffed. "Now listen to me. I want you off this case. And I want you off it now!"

"Are you saying that my sister and grandmother are no longer suspects?"

"I'm saying no such thing."

"In that case, I'm still on the case."

"If you get in my way, I will lock you up. Just because your boyfriend is a cop, that doesn't give you the right—"

"Don't bring Jack into this. I can fight my own battles."

"I meant what I said. Don't get in my way!"

Riley led me back to reception where Grandma was waiting for me. I had thought she looked angry the previous day because of Betty's man-sized sea creatures, but that was nothing compared to how she looked right now. I had no idea that it was possible for anyone's face to turn that shade of red.

"Where have you been?" She screamed at me.

"I've been here for the last hour, but they wouldn't let me see you."

"It's a good job they let me out of there when they did because another five minutes, and I would have turned them all into cockroaches. And then, taken great pleasure in stamping on each of them in turn."

"Come on, let's get out of here." I led the way outside.

"How dare they bring me in for questioning?" she said, as soon as we were outside.

"You can't really blame them, Grandma. You did go into the Wool TV studios, ranting and raving about Lucinda."

"I've explained why I did that. That woman had had the audacity to criticise Everlasting Wool. I was going to give her a piece of my mind."

"What did they say to you?"

"They just asked a lot of stupid questions. Like the police always do. You should know—you're living with one of them."

"Jack's not that bad."

"You've changed your tune. You used to call him every name under the sun."

"That was before I got to know him. Anyway, it's over now. Let's go home."

"It may be over for you, but it certainly isn't over for me. You don't really think I'm going to let them get away with treating me like that, do you?"

"What do you mean?"

"Precisely what I said. No one treats Mirabel Millbright like that and gets away with it."

"You have to promise me that you won't retaliate,

Grandma."

"Why should I?"

"Because if you do, I won't take part in the Levels Competition this year."

"That's blackmail!"

"Correct. Do we have an agreement?"

"I suppose so."

I wasn't entirely sure that I could trust her. Particularly not after what had happened with Betty.

Grandma was still grumbling when I dropped her off at Ever.

***

I parked my car, and began to walk to the office. I hadn't gone more than a few yards when I found my way blocked by a crowd of people, who were gathered around something on the pavement. As I got closer, I realised there was an elderly man lying on the ground.

"What happened?"

"He's dead," someone said. "A heart attack, I think."

I spotted a familiar face in the crowd. It was Lester, and standing next to him was the young woman I'd seen at Aunt Lucy's house. It took me a moment to remember her name—Monica.

"Lester!" I called.

"Oh? Hi, Jill. I didn't see you there."

"What are you up to?"

"Sorry, I can't talk right now."

Then, the penny dropped.

"Of course. Sorry to have interrupted."

I was such an idiot. Lester was now a trainee Grim

Reaper, and this poor man was no doubt one of his—err—I struggled to come up with the right term: clients?

"Concentrate, Lester, please!" Monica admonished him.

"Sorry, Monica." Lester went back to his paperwork.

I figured I wasn't helping Lester by hanging around. It was a difficult enough job without him having to worry about me looking on. I crossed the road, and went on my way. There wasn't enough money in the world to get me to sign up to do that job.

***

As I approached my office building, the woman in front of me squealed, and then tried to grab her hat, which was spiralling upwards. For a moment, I was a little confused because there was no wind to speak of. But then I realised that the hat was being pulled higher and higher by a very thin thread. Sitting on the window ledge of my office was Winky. He was holding what appeared to be a fishing rod. He'd hooked the woman's hat, and was reeling it in. Fortunately, the woman didn't seem to realise what had happened. She presumably thought it had just been blown off.

I hurried upstairs and into the outer office. Waiting for me there was Norman. I'd telephoned him first thing that morning to ask him to come in.

"Norman. I'm sorry to have kept you waiting. Would you mind holding on for just a few more minutes?"

"Sure. No problem."

I burst through the door of my office to find Winky sitting on the sofa. He was wearing the woman's hat, and looking very pleased with himself.

"What do you think you're doing? You can't go around stealing people's hats."

"I was practising my fly fishing. And although I say it myself, I'm getting rather good at it."

"I don't care how good you are. You mustn't do it again."

"You're such a spoilsport. Anyway, what do you think of the hat? Do you think it looks good on me?"

"No I don't. It looks ridiculous."

"How about this one, then?" He reached under the sofa, and brought out another hat—this one had a feather in it.

"No. That looks even worse."

"Really? I thought the feather was rather fetching." Once again, he reached under the sofa. This time, he produced a trilby. "How about this?"

"Yeah. That suits you—" What was I saying? "Never mind the fashion parade. How many hats do you have under there?"

"Twenty-six," he said, proudly.

"This has to stop! You can't go around stealing people's hats like this."

"How else am I supposed to practise fly fishing?"

"You're not. Can't you find a hobby more suited to a cat?"

"Such as?"

"I don't know. Playing with a toy mouse or something?"

"I don't like mice." He shuddered.

"Anyway, this has to stop. What am I supposed to do with all these hats?"

"I thought you could sell them at a car boot sale. We could split the takings sixty-forty."

I used the intercom to ask Jules to send Norman through.

"I'm sorry about the delay, Norman. Take a seat."

"Have you found my bottle tops?"

"Yes, I have, but before I tell you where they are, I need to discuss something else with you first."

"Okay?" He looked a little puzzled, but then Norman always looked a little puzzled.

"Do you ever see Betty Longbottom?"

"No. I haven't seen her in ages."

"She's done something rather silly."

"You mean when she dumped me?"

"No. Something even sillier than that. It was Betty who took your bottle tops."

"Betty? Are you sure?"

"Unfortunately, yes."

"Why would she do that?"

"Did you know that she's opened a shop?"

"No. I didn't. What kind of shop?"

"It's called 'She Sells.' It sells seashells and other marine paraphernalia. It's on the high street."

"I still don't understand why she took my bottle tops."

"She was having money difficulties. I believe she may have sold some of them to help finance the shop."

"If she needed money, why didn't she just ask me?"

"Would you have helped her?"

"Yeah, why not?"

"After the way she dumped you?"

"Yeah, well, she's still a friend, isn't she?"

I was beginning to see Norman in a totally different light. The guy was no rocket scientist, but apparently he had a heart of gold.

"Do you want to take this to the police?"

"The police?" He looked puzzled. "Why would I go to the police?"

"Betty stole from you."

"I suppose she did, but I would have given her the bottle tops anyway, if she'd asked."

Betty Longbottom did not deserve this young man. He was far too good for her.

"Shall I speak to Betty, and arrange for you to meet with her? You can discuss the best way to proceed with this between you."

"Do you think she'll agree to see me?"

Bless.

Chapter 16

Daze had agreed to meet me at Cuppy C. I arrived ten minutes early, and bought myself a cappuccino and a blueberry muffin. I was halfway through the muffin when Daze arrived.

"Morning, Jill. Would you like a top-up?"

"No, I'm okay, thanks."

Daze ordered herself a cup of tea and a round of toast with raspberry jam. I couldn't help but admire Daze's restraint when it came to muffins.

"How did your patrol go in Washbridge Park, on the full moon?" I asked.

"We didn't catch a single rogue werewolf all night. Still, I suppose that's a good thing." She took a sip of her tea.

Thank goodness I'd found Jerry Travers, and taken him back to the Range in Candlefield before Daze and her team had arrived.

"So, what can you tell me about Candlefield Academy of Supernatural Studies?"

"First off, no one calls it that. Everyone knows it as CASS."

"Do you know why you were selected to attend there?"

"No, but then no one ever does. An invitation simply arrives at your door on or around your eleventh birthday."

"That must have been exciting for the eleven-year-old you?"

"Scary, more like. I was terrified. I'd assumed that I'd be going to my local school, but then the invitation arrived, and that changed everything. At first, I didn't want to go, but my parents persuaded me that it was too good an opportunity to pass up. What do they want you to give a talk on?"

"What it's like to be a human."

"I don't understand?" Daze looked puzzled. "You're not a human."

"I'm the closest thing to one they can get. Growing up in the human world, and not knowing that I was a witch, means that I have more insight than most."

"I guess so. Have you said you'll do it?"

"Yes. I didn't see any reason not to. So, what exactly can you tell me about CASS?"

"Where do I begin?"

"Well to start with, where is it, exactly? Aunt Lucy did try to explain—she said it was somewhere in the north?"

"It's located on the very edge of the sup world—miles away from any populated area. It's about as remote as it could be, and is surrounded by thick forests and mountains. The only access is by airship. I hated that airship—I've never been very good with heights."

"Why on earth did they choose to build a school in such a remote spot?"

"They didn't. The building was originally home to Charles Wrongacre, one of the most powerful wizards Candlefield has ever known. When he died, he left the school and land to the Combined Sup Council, to be used in a manner which would best serve the community of wizards and witches.

"Was Wrongacre a level six wizard?"

"This pre-dated the levels structure that we use today. It was all very much simpler back then when there were only four categories: apprentice, practising, master and grandmaster. Wrongacre was one of only two grandmasters—the other was Braxmore."

"Braxmore? I've heard that name before. Grandma mentioned him to me. She said he was rumoured to be TDO's mentor."

"That's him."

"How can that be? That would make him a zillion years old."

"The truth is that no one really knows whether Braxmore is alive or not, but back then there was a bitter rivalry between the two families. Wrongacre stood for everything that was good in Candlefield; Braxmore stood for everything that was evil. Wrongacre is said to have died of a broken heart shortly after his only son was murdered."

"By Braxmore?"

Daze shrugged. "No one knows. Anyway, CASS opened its doors to its first pupils ten years after Wrongacre's death."

"I still find it hard to believe they thought it would be a good place to locate a school."

"The Combined Sup Council thought its remote location would promote learning because there would be none of the everyday distractions that there are in the populated regions of Candlefield. It's a nice theory."

"What do you mean?"

"The kids who go there are still kids. They're going to get up to mischief every now and then regardless of where they are. I know I did."

"Aunt Lucy said there are all kinds of dangerous creatures up there. Dragons and the like?"

"That's right. Do you remember the mystical creatures you read about in fairy tales when you were a kid in the human world? Where do you think those ideas came from?"

"Sups?"

"Precisely. The stories were probably written by sups who'd attended CASS."

"How do they keep the creatures out of the school?"

"It has very high walls which stops most of them."

"Most? What about those creatures that can fly?"

"They can be a problem at times. Life can get pretty interesting at CASS."

"Interesting? It sounds downright dangerous to me. I'm surprised that any parents would allow their children to attend a school located in such a dangerous region."

"Some don't, but CASS is a very prestigious school, and most parents don't want to deny their children the chance to go there. Despite its location, and the dangerous creatures, the school has an excellent safety record. All things considered."

"Very reassuring. Did you enjoy your time there?"

"It was fantastic—probably the best years of my life. Although, when I first arrived there, I was absolutely terrified. So were all the other first year pupils. We'd all been used to living here where there are no scary creatures to worry about. The first time I saw a dragon fly overhead, I nearly peed myself."

It was difficult for me to imagine Daze being scared of anything, but then it was hard to imagine living among dragons.

"Being at CASS is like living in a totally different world. Unless you've actually been there, it's impossible to imagine."

"What about the school itself? Did you enjoy that?"

"Once I'd got used to the idea of boarding, yes. At first, I hated not being able to go home at the end of each day, but I soon got used to it. Everyone does eventually. The teachers were amazing. There were lots of different characters, but they were all brilliant in their own way. And the lessons—I learned so much there. If I ever have children, I hope they get an invitation to go to CASS."

"Wouldn't you be worried about them?"

"Of course I would, but I'd also know that they'd be embarking on the adventure of a lifetime. It isn't just the academic studies, it's the extra-curricular activities too."

"What kind of activities?"

"All kinds of sports, obviously, but so much more. My favourite was the Dragon Club."

"What on earth is that?"

"Occasionally, a dragon's nest would be abandoned, usually because the mother had been killed. The Dragon Club would collect the eggs, and try to incubate them. When the young were born, they'd be raised until they were old enough to be released into the wild."

"You helped to raise a baby dragon?"

"Yeah. Pretty cool, eh?"

"No kidding. The only animals we had at my school were a couple of rats."

"The treasure hunts were pretty cool too."

"We did that kind of stuff at my school."

"I doubt they were the same. These weren't organised by the school—in fact they were frowned upon by the teaching staff. It wasn't exactly 'treasure'—that's just what everyone called it. They were based around the various myths which surrounded Wrongacre."

"The original owner?"

"Not the man. The building which still bore his name."

"What kind of myths?"

"Too many to mention. Some of them were obviously nonsense—presumably made up by the many generations of pupils who had attended the school. But others were true—like the dream-stones."

"Go on. I'm intrigued."

"I have to admit that when I first heard about the dream-stones, I was convinced it was just one of the many fabricated stories that did the rounds. I couldn't have been any more wrong. According to the myth, there are seven dream-stones spread throughout the human and sup worlds. Whoever possesses one of those stones is able to move between the real world and the dream world."

"Whoa. Back up. What do you mean when you say 'dream world'?"

"Its name kind of gives it away. It's the world you get glimpses of when you're asleep."

"But surely dreams are just in my head. They're my self-conscious at work."

"That's what most people believe."

"But you don't?"

"I used to before I knew about the dream-stones. Anyway, as I was saying. There was a myth, or a rumour if you prefer, that one of the dream-stones was hidden within the grounds of Wrongacre. Generations of pupils had tried to find it, but without success."

"Which probably proves it is just a myth."

"Until—"

"Until?"

"Until Edward Hedgelog came along."

"Sorry? Who? Did you say Edward Hedgehog? That has

to be a made-up name."

"Hedgelog not Hedgehog. Unsurprisingly, his nickname was Spikes. He was in my year. I didn't know him particularly well. He was a quiet boy who kept himself to himself. Most of the pupils formed small groups to investigate the myths, but Edward always worked alone."

"And he found it? The dream-stone?"

"Yes. It was during our very last term at CASS—in fact only a few days before we were due to come home for good."

"What happened to him?"

"He came back to Candlefield."

"And?"

"And nothing. I haven't heard anything of him since then."

"So, how do you know the dream-stone stuff is real? You didn't actually see him—err—do anything?"

"No. But there's no doubt in my mind it was real."

"I don't buy it. It sounds crazy to me."

"As crazy as a world where sups live, but that humans can't see?"

"Yes, but—err—that's not the same. Is it?"

Daze shrugged. "When are you going to give your talk?"

"We haven't set a date yet. The headmistress suggested it might be next month."

After Daze had left, I went over to join the twins at a table near to the counter. Although I was glad to have seen the back of the ice maidens, I was conscious of the fact that the twins now had another problem. Having the two rooms upstairs unoccupied meant they had no rental income. That was a situation that couldn't continue for very long because they needed the money to pay their mortgages.

"I guess you'll have to advertise for new tenants." I was eyeing the butterscotch muffin on Amber's plate.

"No need," she said. "We've already got someone."

"Already? How did you manage that?"

"We've let both rooms." Pearl beamed. "Jethro came in here yesterday with three other guys. They overheard us talking about the rooms upstairs, and it just so happened that two of them were looking for new accommodation."

"These guys? Are they by any chance the Sweaty—err—I mean Adrenaline Boys?"

"Yeah. How come you've heard of them?" Amber looked puzzled.

"I don't think I've mentioned it before, but Jethro is now going out with my PA."

"Mrs V?" Now it was Pearl's turn to look puzzled.

"Not Mrs V!" I laughed. "I've now got two PAs. They job-share. It's Jules who's seeing Jethro. She's in her twenties."

"How long has she been going out with him?" Amber finished off her muffin. How mean—she hadn't even offered me a bite.

"Not long. And she may not be going out with him for much longer."

"Why not?"

"Jules isn't very happy that he's taken up dancing again. She didn't want him to join the Adrenaline Boys. Are you sure it's a good idea to give the rooms to those two guys?"

"Why not?"
"What did Alan and William have to say about it?"
"They're okay with it," Pearl said.
"Yeah." Amber nodded. "They don't mind."
"You haven't told them, have you?"
"No, but we will. Soon."
"Yeah. Soon. Real soon."

Chapter 17

I had Audrey Bone's address, so I decided to take the direct approach by turning up at her door. I loved cute house names, but Audrey's house name hardly fell into the cute category. The plaque on the wall read 'The Bone House.'

I rang the bell, and moments later, a woman answered the door.

"Yes? Can I help you?" Her voice was sharp and full of impatience.

"Morning. My name is Jill Gooder. I'd like to ask you a few questions about your sister, Lucinda."

"Are you the police?"

"No. I'm a—"

"If you're not the police, then I have nothing to say to you."

She started to close the door, but I managed to get my foot into the gap.

"Do you mind? Move your foot!"

"My sister, Kathy, works at Wool TV. She's a suspect in your sister's murder. I just want to find out who the real murderer is. Surely, you want to bring that person to justice?"

"I don't see how I can help. Lucinda and I barely saw one another. I've only spoken to her a dozen times in the last five years."

"Is that because of what happened between you and Michael?"

"You seem to know an awful lot about my private life."

"I know that you and he were an item before he married Lucinda."

"You're barking up the wrong tree. Michael and I only ever went out for a short time; it was never very serious. We'd drifted apart long before he met Lucinda. In fact, he didn't even realise she was my sister until they'd been out on a few dates."

"Still, it must have irked when they got together."

"No. It didn't have any effect on me whatsoever. Michael and I were history by then. And besides, even if it had, do you think I would have waited until now to take my revenge?"

"So why did you and Lucinda fall out?"

"There was no particular reason—no flashpoint. I know this will sound awful, but the truth is I didn't like her very much. She wasn't a nice person. She was self-centred, selfish and narcissistic. They say blood is thicker than water, but that's nonsense. You get to pick your friends."

"Can you think of anyone who might have wanted to kill Lucinda?"

"You're asking the wrong person. She and I were practically strangers. And anyway, I thought she'd been murdered by a serial killer. That's what I read in the newspaper. Now, if you don't mind." She gently kicked my foot. "I'd really like you to leave."

I did as she asked.

If what Audrey Bone had just told me was true, then it seemed that she and her sister were virtually strangers. I simply couldn't convince myself that she'd had anything to do with her sister's murder.

***

I stopped off at the local minimarket to pick up a bottle

of ginger beer and a packet of custard creams. While I was in the queue, waiting to pay, I spotted something which I thought might provide Winky with a distraction from his fly fishing obsession.

"How is Armi, Mrs V?" She was knitting a luminous pink scarf, for reasons known only to herself.

"He's getting around better on the crutches, but it looks like we'll just be spectators at the Cuckoo Clock Appreciation Society dinner and dance."

"I'm sorry to hear that. I know how much you were both looking forward to it."

"It's just one of those things." She shrugged. "But still, I do have Woolcon to look forward to. You must be getting excited about that, too?"

"Very." Almost as much as my next dental appointment.

Winky was on the sofa, trying on one hat after another.

"I hope you haven't been fly fishing out of the window again."

"They're not biting, today." He sighed.

This was my opportunity to try out the gadget I'd bought at the minimarket. I slipped the pen-torch out of my pocket, and began to shine it on the dark wooden floor.

"Winky! Look!" I made the light dance across the floor.

"What am I meant to be looking at?"

"The light." I made it dance around a little more.

"Yeah? So what? You've got a torch—big whoop!"

"Cats are meant to go crazy for this kind of thing."

"Are you serious? I think you've been watching too

many YouTube videos. No self-respecting cat would waste his time chasing around the floor after a patch of light. Did you buy that just to try and entertain me?"

"Yeah. I thought you'd like it."

"If you want to spend money on me, why don't you buy more salmon?"

***

When I arrived home that night, I heard voices coming from the lounge. It was Blake and Jen. I immediately feared the worst. Was Jen telling Jack that Blake was a wizard?

"Hi, everyone," I said, nervously.

"Hi, Jill." Blake seemed perfectly relaxed, which I found reassuring.

"Sorry for dropping in unannounced," Jen said. "We actually came over to ask if you wanted to do dinner."

"That sounds like a great idea. When did you have in mind?"

"Well, we had thought tonight," Jen said. "But it looks as though these two now have other plans."

"Oh?"

"Jack's been showing me his trophy," Blake said.

I'd been so concerned about what they might be discussing that I hadn't even noticed Jack's ten-pin bowling trophy, which was standing on the coffee table. He must have rescued it from the spare bedroom.

"I had no idea that Jack was into ten pin bowling," Blake said. "If I'd known, I would have challenged him to a game before now."

"These two have booked a lane for tonight," Jen said.

"You don't mind, do you, Jill?" Jack looked at me with those puppy dog eyes of his. "You and Jen can have a girly night in."

"Okay by me." I shrugged. "Just so long as you guys nip out and buy wine for us before you go."

An hour later, Jen and I were enjoying takeaway pizza. The two guys had gone to the bowling alley. I wasn't sure if I wanted Jack to win or lose—he would be unbearable either way.

We'd almost finished the pizza when there was a knock at the door. It was Mrs Rollo; she had a huge smile on her face.

"I'm sorry to disturb you, Jill. Do you have a moment?"

"I've actually got a visitor just now, Mrs Rollo. Can it wait until later?"

"I just wanted to tell you that I've had exciting news."

Something told me that Mrs Rollo's idea of exciting news, and mine, were a million miles apart.

"I've been invited to appear on Bake TV."

"I've never heard of it."

"It's very popular among the baking crowd. They heard about my recent win with the fruit cake, and want me to take part in the Big Bake Challenge. I thought you might like to come along to the studio where they're recording it, to cheer me on. I've got a few free tickets."

This was a disaster. The only reason that Mrs Rollo had won a trophy for her fruit cake was because I'd replaced her creation with one I'd produced using magic. If I'd realised it would lead to this, I would never have done it. What was I supposed to do now? If I let her go on TV by herself, it would be a disaster. I couldn't let her embarrass herself in that way; she might never get over it.

"Sure. That would be great."

"I'll let you have all the details later. Anyway, I don't want to keep you from your guest, so I'll say goodnight."

Oh bum!

Jen was much better company that night than on the previous occasion when we'd stayed in together. All her doubts and fears concerning Blake seemed to have evaporated. Whenever she did mention him, it was in glowing terms.

It didn't take us long to finish off the bottle of wine which Jack had fetched for us. Jen had drunk rather more than I had.

"We need more of this." She waved the empty bottle at me.

"I can nip down to the shop, if you like?"

"No need." She giggled. "I've got plenty over at my place."

In no time at all, she was back with two more bottles of wine.

Two hours later, and Jen was pretty drunk. I had steadied off some time back, and had encouraged her to do the same, but she was having none of it.

"I really love Blake." She hiccupped.

"He is a really cool guy."

"You have no idea." She laughed. "He's more than just cool, but I can't tell you why. It's a secret." She put a finger to her lips.

"Perhaps you should be getting back home," I suggested.

"No! We're having fun, aren't we?"

"Yes, of course. But it is getting late."

"It's not late." She tapped her watch. "Where's that wine?"

"It's all gone." I lied.

"Boo! That's not fair! If Blake was here, he could magic us a new bottle."

Oh no! This really was not good. I had to get her back home before she said something that she and I might both regret.

"Come on, Jen. I think we should get you home."

"Not yet. The night's still young."

I ignored her protests, took her arm, and led her across the road.

"I'll make coffee." I eased her onto the sofa.

I figured that caffeine might bring her around, but by the time I'd made the drinks, and taken them through to the lounge, she was fast asleep. I had a quick slurp of coffee, and then made my way back across the road.

An hour later, Jack and Blake arrived back.

"Guess who won," Jack said.

"Judging by the stupid expression on your face, I'm guessing you did."

"Where's Jen?" Blake looked around.

"She was tired, so I walked her home."

"Is she okay?"

"Yeah. She's fine."

"I suppose I'd better get back." Blake started for the door. "I demand a rematch soon, Jack."

"Sure. Any time."

I waited until Blake had left, and then said, "There's something I meant to tell Jen. I won't be a minute." I was out of the door before Jack had the chance to ask any questions.

I caught up with Blake just as he was going into his house.

"Blake! Hold on a minute!"

I ushered him inside, and peered into the lounge. Jen was still fast asleep on the sofa.

"What's wrong?" he said.

"Jen had too much to drink."

"Everyone's entitled to get a little tipsy every now and then."

"It's not that. She started talking about magic."

"How do you mean?"

"She said that you'd be able to magic up a bottle of wine for us."

"People say things like that all the time. She probably wasn't talking about actual magic."

"That's not all. She said that you were a cool guy, and that I didn't know just how cool, but that she couldn't tell me because it was a secret."

"Oh dear."

"You have to have a serious talk to her, Blake. You have to make her understand the implications of her telling anyone your secret. It's lucky it was me she said it to. What will happen if she goes drinking with a crowd of human friends, and spills the beans to them?"

"You're right. Sorry, Jill. Don't worry. I'll speak to her."

When I got back to the house, Jack looked concerned. "Is everything okay?"

"Yeah. Everything's fine."

"Why did you go rushing over there?"

"Jen had a little too much wine. That's why I had to take

her home earlier. I just wanted to double-check that she was okay."

"And is she?"

"Yeah. She's fast asleep on the sofa."

"In other news, it would appear that I'm the undisputed king of ten pin bowling." Jack looked smugger than I'd seen him look for some time.

"And yet, you can't beat me."

That wiped the grin off his face.

"Oh, by the way, Jill. I bumped into Mr Hosey on the way in from work. He was riding around on that silly little train of his."

"I saw him too. You'll never guess what he asked me." I laughed. "He wanted to know if we'd like to go to his open house—to see his silly little train set. Can you imagine?"

"Yeah— about that—there's something I need to tell you."

"Please tell me you didn't."

"I think I may have."

"May have? Have you or have you not told him we'll go over there?"

"He caught me off guard."

"Jack! Have you said we'll go over there?"

"It's your fault."

"How is it my fault?"

"He said it was a pity we were going to visit my brother on Tuesday. I said we weren't. That's when he said—"

"Well that's just fantastic. What better way to spend an evening than at Mr Hosey's. I'll probably never speak to you again."

***

"Amber! Wait for me! Pearl! Wait!"

They were ahead of me in the corridor. The walls felt as though they were closing in on me.

"Amber! Pearl!"

Neither of them looked back. Even though they were only walking, I couldn't catch up with them, no matter how fast I ran.

"Please, girls! Wait for me!"

They came to a staircase.

"Don't go down there!"

They paid no heed to my words. By the time I reached the top of the stairs, they were nowhere to be seen. I took the stairs two at a time. When I reached the bottom, the twins were standing in front of a door. There was danger behind that door—I was sure of it.

"Amber! Don't open that door! Pearl, stop her!"

Amber turned around to face me. "It's okay, Jill. There's nothing to worry about."

"No! Amber, it's dangerous! Don't open that door! Pearl, you have to stop her!"

Amber turned the handle.

"Jill! Wake up!"

I sat up in bed.

"Are you okay?" Jack said.

"What? Yeah."

"You've been having another nightmare. You said something about a door."

"I don't remember." I did—only too clearly.

"You said 'don't open that door'."

"It must have been the door to Mr Hosey's house. I dreamt that we had to go over there to see his trainset. Oh, wait, that's not a dream; it's real. Some idiot agreed that we would."

"You're never going to let me forget about that, are you?"

"Nope. I never am. Unless of course, you can think of some way to make it up to me."

"Hmmm. I might have a few ideas." He pulled me into his arms.

Chapter 18

For reasons that are none of your business, I was a little later than usual setting off for work. As I drove up the high street, I noticed there was scaffolding outside She Sells. The van parked on the pavement, had the name Speedy Signs on the side. My curiosity was piqued, so I found somewhere to park, and then walked back down to Betty's shop.

Inside, was the woman herself: Betty Longbottom. She didn't look very pleased with life.

"Morning, Betty."

"Oh, it's you." She scowled.

"What's wrong? What did I do?"

"You told Norman that I'd stolen his bottle tops."

"What did you expect me to do? You can't go around stealing other people's property."

"They were only bottle tops."

"They were *Norman's* bottle tops. And from all accounts, some of them were quite valuable. Anyway, I got the impression that he wasn't going to press charges."

"Of course he's not. Norman is still infatuated with me."

"So, why are you in such a foul mood?"

"Because, although he isn't going to press charges, he wants to come into the business with me."

"I suppose that's only fair. It was partly his money which allowed you to open the shop in the first place."

"He wants us to sell bottle tops!"

"Oh dear." I laughed. "Is that why you're having the sign changed?"

"Yes. The shop is now going to be called 'Sea Shells and

Bottle Tops'."

"It has a certain ring to it."

"Do you know how long it took me to come up with the name: She Sells? A long time, that's how long. It was the perfect name, and now I've had to change it. I hope you're satisfied."

The woman was unbelievable. She'd stolen from Norman, and yet he'd forgiven her, and still she wasn't happy.

Sheesh! Some people!

***

"I'm going to kill that man." My mother appeared, unannounced, in the office. Winky hissed at her before disappearing under the sofa.

"Which man would that be?" I had a sneaking suspicion that I already knew the answer to that question, but I thought I'd tease her. "Alberto?"

"No! Not Alberto. I'm talking about that father of yours."

"What's he done now?"

"He did it on purpose."

My mother was nothing if not cryptic.

"What did he do?"

"He's only gone and bought a house on the same street as me and Alberto."

"Oh? Maybe he didn't realise you lived there?"

"Don't try to stick up for him, Jill. He knew perfectly well that we lived there."

"Have you spoken to him about it?"

"Speak to him? I don't ever intend to speak to that man

again! That's why I'm here. I thought you could have a word with him."

"Me? I don't think I should interfere."

"Come on, Jill. He'll listen to you. He said he wanted to make it up to you for not being there when you were growing up."

"Yes, but this would be taking advantage."

"So?"

"Okay, I'll have a word with him, but I can't promise anything."

"Do your best because I won't be responsible for my actions if he and his bit of skirt move in."

And with that, she took her leave.

There was a time when I didn't have to worry about ghosts or talking cats. Little had I realised back then, just how fortunate I'd been.

The door to my office flew open, and in walked two of the scariest objects I'd ever seen. Leading the way was a giant ball of green wool with skinny, red legs. Following behind it, was a giant knitting needle.

"What do you think, Jill?" the ball of wool said.

Before I could say anything, the knitting needle jumped in, "These costumes are great, aren't they?"

Having heard the voices, at least I now knew that this wasn't a horrible spell cast by Grandma as retribution for some perceived slight. This was much worse: It was Mrs V and Jules in their Woolcon costumes.

"You're not actually going to wear those on the day, are you?"

"Of course we are," Mrs V, the ball of wool, said.

"I think we look cool," Jules, the knitting needle, agreed.

Out of the corner of my eye, I spotted Winky, sitting on the sofa. He was shaking his head—no doubt in total disbelief at what he saw.

"There's still time for you to get a costume, Jill," the knitting needle said. "We thought you could go as a crochet hook."

"Not a chance! I told you when I agreed to go to Woolcon that I wasn't going to wear fancy dress."

"But everyone will be in costume."

"Not everyone. I won't, for a start."

"You're a spoilsport." The ball of wool admonished me. "Come on, Jules. Jill is just a killjoy."

The ball of wool and knitting needle both squeezed through the door, and went back into the outer office.

"Do you think we're safe from the crazy in here?" Winky said.

***

Something was bugging me. When I'd had the run-in with Leo Riley, I'd asked him whether they were treating the two poisonings as being linked. As always, he'd been evasive, and had given me a 'no comment' response.

This was crucial to the whole case. If the two murders had been committed by the same person, that should make it easier to prove that Kathy hadn't been involved. I needed to find out what was happening with the police investigation into both murders. Had they linked them? And if not, why not?

Asking Leo Riley would have been a complete waste of time. If I wanted to find out what was going on inside Washbridge police station then I was going to have to get inside there, and take a look for myself.

The first time I'd ever used magic to get inside the police station was shortly after Jack had moved to the area. I'd been investigating what had then been known as the Animal Serial Killer murders. On that occasion, I'd come very close to being discovered, and had had to hide under the desk at the front of the incident room. It was the first time I'd seen Jack's Tweety Pie socks.

The process of getting inside the police station was much easier for me now because I'd done it so many times before. Also, the fact that I was no longer restricted to only thirty minutes of invisibility was a great help. I was now able to become invisible at will for long periods of time.

Once inside the building, I made my way past the reception desk, and then waited until someone opened the door so I could follow them into the main building. Once there, I made my way upstairs to where I knew the incident rooms were located. The first one I came to was deserted. After checking to make sure there was no one in the corridor, I pushed the door open and went inside. It was obvious from the photos on the whiteboards that I was in the right room. It was the same room I'd been in when I'd had to hide from Jack. One whiteboard showed details of Lucinda Gray's murder. The other one had details of the murder of a Mr Lucas Wright—the first poisoning victim. Lucinda had died almost instantly after drinking water that had been laced with a quick-acting poison. The other victim had also died after drinking water that had been poisoned, but his death had been much slower. According to the notes on the whiteboard, it had taken over an hour for him to die. The poisons used in the two murders had obviously been very different.

Although their names meant nothing to me, the notes written beside them seemed quite significant. The one used to kill the first victim was readily available at most hardware stores, but the one which had been used to kill Lucinda was available only in commercial laboratories. That at least explained why the police hadn't linked the two cases. It would be very unusual for the same killer to use two such different poisons. Unusual but not unheard of.

I was about to make my exit when I heard voices and footsteps. They were headed my way. But there was no reason to panic—I was still invisible. I hurried over to the door, and waited. Moments later, a number of police officers, led by Leo Riley, came through the door. Before it closed behind them, I managed to sneak out.

***

I dreaded to think what kind of affair Deli and Nails' wedding would be. I'd seen the way Deli dressed, and I'd seen Nails in action. I had a horrible vision of him clipping his toenails while waiting for his bride to walk down the aisle. I'd pleaded with Jack to let me decline the invitation, but he was determined to go to what would no doubt be the Wedding of the Year.

I hadn't seen Mad for a while, so rather than post the reply, I'd decided to deliver it to her at the library.

Unsurprisingly, she wasn't behind the front desk. Instead, I found her in her favourite hiding place—the stock room at the back of the building.

"I thought I'd find you here."

"Jill! You scared me to death."

"You're a Ghost Hunter. How can I possibly scare you?"

"What brings you to this hive of activity?"

"I brought you this." I handed over the envelope.

Mad grinned. "Is this what I think it is?"

"I'm afraid so. I'll be honest with you, I wanted to make an excuse not to go, but Jack wouldn't hear of it. He says he wants to meet more of my friends. It turns out I'm living with the only man in Washbridge who actually likes weddings."

"Don't worry, Jill. After he's been to my mother's, he'll never want to go to another one in his life."

"I don't suppose there's any chance that your mother and Nails will fall out and call it off, is there?"

"I live in hope. You should see the monstrous bridesmaid's dress she wants me to wear."

"I hadn't thought of that. Seeing you in a bridesmaid's dress might actually make the day bearable." I laughed. "I can see that your library duties are keeping you busy as usual."

"Oh yeah. I'm run off my feet."

"What about the ghost hunting? How's that going?"

"Still very busy. There's something strange going on in Washbridge. Something which is attracting more and more ghosts from Ghost Town, but I have no idea what it is. Even with Henry to help, we're still struggling."

"Oh yeah, I meant to ask. How are you and Henry getting along?"

"Really well." Mad had a wicked smile. "And, I do mean 'really well'."

"I think it's time I met this guy of yours. Maybe we should have a night out; the four of us."

"I'd be up for that, and I'm sure Henry would."

"Great. I'll have a word with Jack, and give you a call."

***

On my way home, I decided to call in on Kathy to see how she was bearing up. I knew she'd still be anxious about the Lucinda Gray case, so thought it best to bring her up to speed—not that I had much to tell her.

Peter made tea for all of us while I spoke to Kathy.

"How are you doing?" I asked. It was a stupid question because I could see that she wasn't coping well.

"I just want this over with. It seems like it's been going on forever. I feel like I have the Sword of Damocles hanging over me—knowing at any moment that they could turn up and take me away."

"I did find out something interesting earlier today. The poison that killed Lucinda, and the poison used in the earlier murder were very different. That's why the police haven't linked the two cases yet."

Just then, there was a knock at the door; Peter went to answer it.

"It's Mandy Drake from Wool TV. She'd like a word with you, Kathy. Do you want to talk to her?"

"Yes. Bring her through." Kathy turned to me, and said, "She's one of the production assistants."

"Hey, Kathy." The woman followed Peter into the room. "I'm sorry to trouble you at home."

"It's okay, Mandy. Come and sit down. This is my sister, Jill."

"Pleased to meet you," I said.

"Would you like a drink, Mandy?" Peter offered. "I was

just making tea."

"No, thanks. I can't stay long. They asked me to come and tell you that they've taken on a news anchor from Needles TV."

I knew how much Kathy had wanted that job, so I expected her to be disappointed, but she just shrugged.

"It's probably for the best. I'm not ready for that responsibility yet."

"When will you be coming back?" Mandy asked.

"I don't know. While I have this thing hanging over me, I'm not sure I can."

"Have you heard any more from the police?"

"Not really. Jill is a private investigator. She's been looking into the murder too."

"I haven't made much headway so far," I said.

"Have you spoken to Donna Proudlove?"

"Yeah. Why do you ask about her in particular?"

"I probably shouldn't tell you this, but I saw Donna and Lucinda having a stand-up slanging match on the morning of the day of the murder."

"Could you hear what it was about?"

"No. But they were really going at it."

Mandy left not long after that. I said my goodbyes thirty minutes later. I was intrigued by what Mandy had said about Donna Proudlove. Perhaps her relationship with Lucinda hadn't been quite as cordial as Donna had led me to believe. Maybe I should have another word with her tomorrow.

Chapter 19

I'd spent the last ten minutes trying to avoid Mrs Mopp and her vacuum cleaner. At least this time both Jack and I had been up and dressed by the time she arrived. We would have been in serious trouble otherwise.

"I'm off," I called to Jack.

He came to the door, and gave me a quick peck on the lips.

"I really don't know why you make out that Mrs Mopp is so difficult to get along with," he said. "She seems perfectly nice to me."

"Are you sure we're talking about the same woman?"

"I just asked her if she'd mind ironing my shirts."

"Are you crazy? I'm surprised you're still breathing."

"She was perfectly nice, and said she'd be delighted to do it."

"Were they her exact words?"

"More or less. Your problem, Jill, is that you don't have any people skills."

"Apparently not."

I tried to contact Donna Proudlove by phone, but all my calls went straight to voicemail. I needed to talk to her sooner rather than later, so I decided to go straight over to the Wool TV studios. She would have to come out eventually. I hid behind one of the pillars closest to the entrance. It was freezing cold, and like a fool, I wasn't wearing a coat. If Donna didn't show up soon, I'd probably die of hypothermia.

It was just before midday, and I was so busy blowing my hands to try to warm them that I almost missed her.

"Donna! Hold on!"

"Jill? What are you doing here?"

"I wanted a word. I've called you several times."

"Sorry, I've been rushed off my feet. Could it wait? I'm in a bit of a hurry just now. Maybe I could call you later?"

She wasn't going to fob me off that easily. I ushered her back inside.

"This won't take long." I led the way over to the seating area.

"What's wrong, Jill? I told you everything I knew last time."

"You didn't tell me that you'd had a blazing row with Lucinda on the morning of the day she was murdered."

"Who told you?"

"That doesn't matter. What was going on between you and Lucinda on that day?"

"It was nothing."

"That's not what I heard. You might as well tell me because I'm going to find out one way or another."

Donna took a seat. "I thought she was my friend. I assumed when she got the job offer that she'd take me with her."

"I take it she wasn't going to do that?"

"No. She told me about the job—she was really excited. And I was excited for her too. I said, 'When do we leave?' She said, '*We* don't'."

"Did she say why she wasn't going to take you with her?"

"She said, 'New job, new start.' When I asked her, 'What about me?' She just shrugged, like I didn't matter. And then I realised that I didn't. Not to her, at least. It's my own fault. I should have known that she'd stab me in the back sooner or later. She'd done it plenty of times before to other people."

"How do you mean? Who else had she done it to?"

"It's what Lucinda did. If you crossed her, or if she no longer needed you, she'd cast you aside like a pair of old socks. She did it to one of the make-up girls, Sally-Ann West. And to one of the cameramen, Giles Lingard. There was a photographer too—I can't remember his name. I'm an idiot. I'd managed to convince myself that I was indispensable to her. Boy, did I get that wrong!"

"No wonder you were angry."

"Of course I was angry, but I didn't kill her if that's what you're thinking."

"You were in the studio on the day she died, and you had more access to her than anyone else."

"Look!" She stood up. "I don't care if you believe me or not. I did not kill Lucinda!"

Where did that leave me with the Lucinda Gray case? So far, I'd spoken to her ex-husband, Michael, who hadn't come across as a murderer. The man had seemed much too wishy-washy to do anything like that. But he did have access to commercial chemicals and poisons, and that meant he had to be a strong suspect. Then there was Lucinda's boyfriend, Callum. There was no obvious reason why he would have wanted Lucinda dead. The only thing I found a little disconcerting about him was that he seemed untouched by his girlfriend's recent death. Donna Proudlove was certainly annoyed at Lucinda who had been all set to dump her young personal assistant. Donna had definitely been angry enough to do something stupid, but had she had the means? The poison used was only available in commercial laboratories, so probably not. Audrey Bone had long since washed her hands of her sister. I'd all but ruled her out of my thinking.

***

"Please, Jack!" I begged.

"No, Jill, I'm not going to lie for you."

"But it's only a small, white lie."

"If you didn't want to see Mrs Rollo's TV show, you shouldn't have offered to go."

"I know. I suppose I'm just going to have to suck it up. What will you be doing while I'm going through that purgatory?"

"Oh, I don't know. Maybe, I'll watch some TV. I might even order in takeaway. Or I might give Blake a call, and ask if he wants to go for a drink."

Jack was enjoying this way too much for my liking. He'd be sorry—I'd get my revenge. Much as I would have liked to have given the baking programme a miss, I owed it to Mrs Rollo not to let her make a fool of herself on TV.

There was a knock at the door. The hour had come.

"I'll get it," Jack said with a huge smirk on his face. "It's Mrs Rollo," he shouted.

"Mrs Rollo? I didn't realise your daughter and grandson would be coming with us."

As if this evening wasn't already bad enough, now I had to contend with that loathsome little brat, Justin.

Mrs Rollo was dressed to the nines, and looked as though she had an audience with the Queen.

"I couldn't let Sheila and Justin miss my big night, could I?" She beamed.

"I guess not."

We took my car to the TV station. Mrs Rollo sat beside me; Sheila and the little monster sat in the back. He never stopped talking all the way there. I was so tempted to use the 'sleep' spell on him, but didn't think his mother or grandmother would approve.

Once at the TV station, Mrs Rollo was escorted backstage while the three of us were shown to the studio from where the programme was to be broadcast.

"You sit between Jill and Mummy, Justin. And you mustn't talk once the programme has started."

"Are you sure you wouldn't rather sit next to me, Sheila?" I offered. Anything to put some distance between me and the little monster.

"No, I'm okay here."

Every time I looked at Justin, he stuck his tongue out at me. The temptation to turn him into a worm was almost too strong to resist.

Half an hour later, a man dressed in an evening suit walked to the front of the set.

"Ladies and gentlemen. Thank you for joining us tonight. In a few minutes, we will begin the programme. I'm sure that most of you are already familiar with the format of the Big Bake Challenge, but for those of you who aren't, I'll quickly run through the rules."

It took the man another fifteen minutes to explain the format of the show, which essentially came down to whoever baked the best cake would be the winner. A few minutes later, the title music played, and the three contestants walked onto the set. They each stood behind their own table, which was already full of baking equipment and ingredients. The host, a man named Jake

Lake, introduced the three contestants. Mrs Rollo was up against Arthur Black, a slim man in his mid-forties. His permanent smile was already beginning to grate on me. The third contestant was Connie Bradshaw who was around the same age as Mrs Rollo. Connie was as miserable as Arthur was happy. Mrs Rollo, meanwhile, looked like a rabbit caught in the headlights.

The compère introduced the two judges who would determine the evening's winner. I'd never heard of either of them, but judging by the round of applause they received from the audience, I could only assume that they were minor celebrities of some kind. The contestants were to bake an almond and raisin cake.

The compere counted down, "Three, two, one. Off you go!"

As the three contestants mixed the ingredients, the judges walked from one table to the next, making notes as they went. As the programme proceeded, I noticed that the judges kept whispering to one another. They appeared to be pointing at Mrs Rollo's handiwork. It was quite obvious that they found her efforts amusing.

Eventually, the time came for the contestants to put their cakes into the ovens. While they were baking, the compère introduced a feature which had been pre-recorded earlier. Essentially, it followed the fortunes of the contestant who had won the show the previous year. While most of the audience were watching the feature, I was studying the two judges who by now had moved into a small cubicle to the right of the set. Both of them were laughing, and it didn't take a genius to know what they were laughing at.

The time came for the three contestants to take their

cakes out of the ovens. If I didn't act now, Mrs Rollo would be a laughing stock. I couldn't allow that to happen, so I cast a spell which would result in the perfect almond and raisin cake.

The three contestants placed their creations on the tables in front of them. The judges started on the far right hand side with Arthur Black. They both scribbled something into their notebooks, and then moved on to Connie Bradshaw. Finally, they walked over to Mrs Rollo's table. The expression on their faces was priceless. They exchanged glances, and then looked again at the cake in disbelief.

After a few minutes of conferring, the two judges passed a note to the compère.

"Ladies and gentlemen. We have a decision. I'm pleased to announce that the winner of this month's Big Bake Challenge is Mrs Rita Rollo."

Mrs Rollo's face lit up. Sheila and Justin stood up, and began to cheer. The rest of the audience followed suit.

On the way home in the car, Mrs Rollo was beside herself with excitement. "I didn't think I stood a chance. I thought I'd got the mixture all wrong."

"It was perfect, Mum," Sheila said. "Don't you think so, Jill?"

"Absolutely perfect." I was just relieved the ordeal was over.

"I wonder what cake I'll have to bake in the next round," Mrs Rollo said.

Oh bum!

Chapter 20

"What's that you're wearing," I called to Jack. I was halfway through my bowl of corn flakes. He was just heading out the door.

"You've seen this suit before."

"I'm talking about the shirt. You always wear white. I didn't even know you had a pink shirt."

"I just fancied a change. I've got to run. See you tonight."

I smelled a rat. Jack would never go to work in a pink shirt. I went upstairs, and checked his wardrobe. There wasn't a white shirt to be seen. Where were they? And then I remembered, Mrs Mopp had said she was going to iron them for him. Or at least, that's what he'd told me she'd said.

I checked the laundry basket, but they weren't in there. Where else could they be? And then it came to me. I went around to the back of the house. There in the dustbin were six white shirts all of which had iron-shaped scorch marks on them. I guessed that was Mrs Mopp's way of telling Jack that she didn't do ironing.

If only he'd had 'people skills' he would have been all right. Snigger.

On my way into work, The Bugle's headline caught my eye.

'Washbridge poisoner strikes again.'

I nipped into the newsagent, and bought a copy. A third victim had been found. Just like the first two, he had died after drinking poisoned water. The man's name was Albert Jackson. He was an accountant, and had been found dead at his desk by his assistant.

A horrible thought crossed my mind. I rushed back into the shop.

"Excuse me. Do you keep back copies of The Bugle?"

"Only for a few days. Why?"

"You don't happen to have the issue which featured the first poison murder, do you?"

"Hold on a minute. I'll just go and check."

He disappeared into the back, but returned only a few moments later.

"There you go. That's on the house."

Once outside, I quickly skimmed the article. In the last paragraph, it mentioned that the victim had been an accountant.

My blood ran cold.

I got straight on the phone, and called Luther's office.

"This is the office of Luther stone, accountant, Cindy speaking. How may I help you today?"

"Hi. Can I speak to Luther, please?"

"Mr Stone isn't here at the moment. Can I take a message?"

"No. This is very urgent. Do you know where Luther is?"

"Who's calling, please?"

"This is Jill Gooder. I'm a client of his."

"I'm afraid Luther hasn't turned in today."

"Is he ill?"

"I don't know. He has appointments for today, but I haven't heard from him. I've tried to call him on his mobile a few times, but there's no answer."

"Do you have his landline number?"

"Yes, but I'm not supposed to call that."

"This may be a matter of life and death. Have you seen today's paper?"

"I never read the newspapers. I prefer the celebrity gossip magazines."

"Two accountants have been murdered in Washbridge over the last few days."

"Goodness. I had no idea. Do you think Luther might be in danger?"

"It's possible. That's why I need you to give me his landline number, right now."

"Shouldn't I call the police?"

"That'll take too long. Just give me his number!"

Cindy hesitated for a moment, but then gave it to me. When I called, I got his answerphone. I tried again several times with the same result. I was wasting time. I had to get over there straight away. I didn't normally like to use magic to travel around the human world unless it was an emergency. It was perfectly possible that Luther was simply ill, but I couldn't take that chance. Not with two accountants dead already. I had to make sure that Luther didn't become victim number three. If that wasn't an emergency, I didn't know what was. I cast the spell, and the next moment, I was standing outside my old flat. I could hear singing coming from inside, and wondered who was living there. But there was no time for that right now.

I knocked on Luther's door. "Luther! Are you in there?"

There was no reply.

"Luther! It's Jill! Open the door!"

There was still no reply. Call it instinct if you like, but something told me that all was not well. I couldn't afford to waste any more time, so I cast the 'power' spell, then forced open the door.

Luther was lying on the floor in the lounge. Next to him was a water bottle which had spilled its contents onto the carpet.

"Luther!" I checked his pulse. It was weak, but at least he was still alive.

I grabbed my phone, and called an ambulance.

The paramedics arrived ten minutes later, and rushed Luther out to the ambulance.

"Will he be okay?"

The paramedic didn't answer.

"Can I come with you?"

"Are you family?"

"No, but—"

"Sorry—only family allowed."

I followed in my car, and sat in the waiting room for over three hours. Eventually, the nurse, who I'd been pestering every fifteen minutes, came to tell me that Luther was going to be okay.

"Can I see him?"

"No, sorry, he's resting. He should be fine by the morning."

I was just on my way out of the hospital when I bumped into Leo Riley on his way in.

"Hold your horses!" He held up his hand. "Where do you think you're going?"

"I was just coming to see you, actually."

"What's going on here? How come you knew about this guy?"

"I think I might know who's behind the poisonings. Two of them, at least. The first one and this one."

"Who?"

"You need to find a man named Robert Roberts."

"Robert Roberts? Is that even a real name?"

"Yes. He used to be my accountant, but I think he may have turned serial killer."

"Is this some kind of joke?"

"No. I'm deadly serious. There isn't time to explain. Just find him! I'm pretty sure you'll find the poison there too."

***

I got home before Jack, and was enjoying a cup of coffee in the lounge when I heard him come through the door.

"Hi!" he called, and then rushed straight upstairs.

What was he up to? I scampered after him.

"What are you doing?"

"Nothing." Could a man look any more guilty?

"What's that behind your back?"

"What?"

"That big bag."

"Oh, this? I've just been doing a bit of shopping."

"What for?"

"Nothing much. Just this and that."

"Show me."

"You wouldn't be interested."

"Show me."

He sighed, and then passed me the bag.

"White shirts. One, two, three, four, five, six of them."

"The others were beginning to look a little worn."

"So it wasn't the iron-shaped scorch marks on the front, then?"

"You've seen them?"

"Oh, yeah."

"I'm sure it was just an accident."

"Of course. As you said, Mrs Mopp is such a sweet little darling. She would never do anything like that on purpose. Especially not to you—what with your people skills and all."

***

I continued to give him a hard time about the shirts over dinner, but then later, the reality of what we were about to face hit me.

"This is all your fault!" I yelled at him.

"How many times do I have to say I'm sorry?"

"However many times you say it, it won't be enough."

"You might actually enjoy tonight."

I glared at him.

"All right." He winced under my gaze. "Not *enjoy*, exactly. But, you might find it interesting."

"Are you being serious? What could I possibly find interesting about Mr Hosey's toy train set?"

"We don't have to stay long. We'll just put in an appearance. Then we can sneak away."

"Is five minutes long enough?"

"Come on, let's go. We may as well get this over with."

It wasn't fair. I was supposedly the most powerful witch in all of Candlefield, and yet I couldn't come up with a spell that would get me out of this.

It was the first time I'd actually seen Mr Hosey's house. On the wall, next to the door, was what appeared to be an old railway station sign. The name on it read, 'Hosey Villas.'

"Hosey Villas? Give me a break!"

Jack shushed me. "He might hear."

"Just ring the bell, Jack. Let's get this over with."

Moments later, Mr Hosey opened the door. He was dressed in what looked like a train driver's uniform complete with peaked hat. He even had a little whistle hanging around his neck.

"Jack and Jill! I'm so glad you could make it."

"We're a little late, sorry," Jack said.

Not late enough as far as I was concerned.

"Not to worry. Take off your shoes, please, and then follow me up to the attic."

We had to scramble up a little ladder, which was quite painful to my stockinged feet.

"Where are the others?" Jack asked once we were standing in the attic.

"It doesn't look as though they're coming." Mr Hosey crawled underneath the train layout to get to the centre section, where all the controls were located.

"How many people did you invite?" I asked.

"At least a dozen. Most of them said they'd be here. I guess something must have cropped up."

"Why didn't we have something crop up?" I whispered to Jack.

"Before I start the demonstration," Mr Hosey said. "I expect you'd like me to talk you through the history of my collection."

"No need for that." I jumped in before Jack could say something which I'd regret. "We're happy just to see the trains go around and around."

Mr Hosey looked horrified. "My trains do not go *'around and around.'* The tracks are laid out in an authentic fashion based on the local rail infrastructure."

Oh boy!

"And anyway," he continued. "It's no trouble to talk you through the history of my collection. I quite enjoy talking about it."

He certainly did. The next sixty-seven minutes, and yes I did time it, he spoke non-stop about his train set. The last time I'd been so bored was when as a kid I'd been forced to attend a lecture on subatomic particles, which in retrospect had been much more interesting than the history of Mr Hosey's train set.

"What?" I jumped when Jack nudged my arm.

"You were falling asleep," he whispered.

"How much longer is this going to last?" I whispered back.

Jack shrugged.

Boy, did he owe me big time for this.

"And now," Mr Hosey said. "For the moment you've all been waiting for."

"Are we finished?" I turned towards the trap door.

"No. We're just starting." He threw the switch, and one of the little trains pulled away from the platform.

Two hours later, Jack and I were walking back to our house.

"It wasn't all that bad, was it?" Jack said.

I stopped, and turned to face him. "Are you having a laugh?"

"Once the trains started to run, I thought it was okay."

"It wouldn't have been quite so bad if we could have just watched the trains going around and around. It was his commentary that drove me insane. Who cares about the rolling stock or the signals? Not me—that's who.

You're going to have to work very hard to make up for this night."

"We'd better get back then, so I can make a start." He grinned.

As we turned onto our street, we bumped into Jen and Blake who were all smiles.

"Hi there," Blake called.

"You two look pleased with life," I said.

"We've had a great night." Jen put her arm through Blake's. "Haven't we, sexy?"

"Yeah. We went for a meal at that new Portuguese restaurant up the road. Then we went to see a movie. It was Jen's idea."

"We had to get out of the house in case that crazy train guy came around."

"Do you mean Mr Hosey?" I said.

"Yeah. That's him. The guy who drives that silly train around. This idiot volunteered us to go and see his train set tonight. Hosey was having an open house or something. When Blake told me, I said there was no way I was going around there, so we decided to go out for the night instead—in case he came looking for us. Who in their right mind would want to spend an evening with Mr Hosey and his train set?"

Who indeed?

Chapter 21

I was just on my way out of the door when my phone rang. It was Peter.

"Have you seen the news this morning, Jill?"

"No. Why?"

"They've arrested someone, and charged them with two of the poisoning murders, but not with Lucinda Gray's. Do you know anything about it?"

"Yeah. I suspect the man they've arrested is my old accountant, Robert Roberts. Did they give his name?"

"No, they didn't. Look, there's another reason I called you. Kathy's gone into work this morning."

"Is that a good idea?"

"I don't think so, but she said she was going stir crazy in the house. I tried to persuade her to give it a few more days, but she wouldn't have it. You know how she can be sometimes."

I did. She was almost as obstinate as I was.

"Would you look in on her, Jill? Just to make sure she's okay."

"Of course. I'll call in on my way into work."

I parked just down the road from Ever, and then walked up the high street. Betty and Norman's shop now had the new sign displayed. I couldn't help but think that particular partnership was doomed.

Kathy was behind the counter when I arrived at Ever.

"Has Peter sent you here?"

"No. What makes you think that?"

"Because I know him. He's been nagging me all morning not to come into work."

"It's only because he's worried about you."

"So he did ask you to check on me?"

"He called me, yes. What are you doing here, anyway?"

"I couldn't stand to be in that house for another minute. It got so bad that I'd rather face your grandmother than stay at home for another day."

"Are you sure I can't talk you into going home?"

"*I'm* sure you can't!" Grandma interrupted. She must have been in the back office. I hadn't heard her creep up on us.

"Kathy shouldn't be at work," I protested.

"Don't speak for me," Kathy said.

"Yes, don't speak for your sister." Grandma joined Kathy behind the counter. "If she says she's okay to come back to work, then she's okay to come back to work, aren't you, dear?" She put her arm around Kathy.

"I'm fine." Kathy flinched, and edged away from Grandma.

"Okay. Just don't overdo it, Kathy. I expect you to keep an eye on her, Grandma."

"Don't you worry," Grandma said. "I'll keep an eye on her, and if she starts to slack off, I'll crack the whip."

***

As soon as I saw the poster in the newsagent's window, I rushed inside, practically trampling two teenagers underfoot.

"Yes, deary?" The woman behind the counter greeted me with a smile. She was wearing odd earrings: The one in her left ear was a penguin, the one in her right ear was an umbrella. I didn't quite get the connection.

"A copy of Biscuit Barrel Monthly, please."

"Sorry, deary, we sold out of those yesterday. It's that competition. Everybody wants to enter it."

"Do you know where I might get a copy?"

"No idea, deary." She shook her head. "I think you might struggle."

Typical! Just my luck. The competition was to win a year's supply of custard creams, and it looked like I was going to miss out.

"Nice of you to show up." Winky looked over the magazine he was reading. "I didn't realise you'd decided to go part-time."

I didn't have the patience to deal with his impertinence, so I ignored him, and began to catch up with some paperwork—mostly bills.

Thirty minutes later, Winky was still engrossed in his magazine.

"What's that you're reading? A flyfishing magazine?"

"No." He lifted it up so I could see the cover.

"Biscuit Barrel Monthly? How did you manage to get hold of a copy?"

"It's not difficult when you know how."

"Do you think I could borrow it when you've done reading it?"

"Of course. Just as soon as I've finished my entry for this competition."

"Which competition?"

"To win a year's supply of custard creams."

"Since when did you like custard creams?"

"I don't, but I figured I could sell them to you."

"Sell them? After all the things I do for you?"

"You're right. I'll only charge you half price."

I got up from my desk, and walked over to the sofa.

"If you don't let me have that magazine so that I can enter the competition, you'll never get another tin of salmon from me again."

"Sheesh! Who gave you a sense of humour bypass? If you must know, I spent all yesterday trying to find this magazine just so you could enter the competition." He passed it to me.

Now I felt bad. I'd obviously misjudged him. "I'm sorry, Winky. That was ungrateful of me."

"I may find it in my heart to forgive you, but it's going to cost you salmon for the rest of the week."

"Okay."

"Red not pink, obviously."

"Obviously."

***

The intercom buzzed.

"Jill, Mr Stone is here to see you. He doesn't have an appointment."

"That's okay, Jules. Send him through, would you?"

Luther looked a thousand times better than he had the last time I'd seen him.

I went to greet him at the door, but he ignored my outstretched hand, and pulled me in for a hug.

"Thank you for saving my life, Jill."

"You're looking a lot better. Are you sure you should be up and about yet?"

"Yes. The hospital discharged me. I still feel a little weak, but it's nothing. If you hadn't come around when you did, I wouldn't be here."

"When I called your office, and they said you hadn't turned in, I feared the worst."

"How did you know?"

"When Robert Roberts came to see me, he was acting very strangely, and said some weird things. I didn't think much about it at the time, but then there was that business with the letter, which I'd supposedly sent to you to cancel our arrangement. When I discovered that two of the people who had been poisoned were accountants, I immediately thought of him. I knew that if my suspicions were right, you would be on his list of targets. That's why I called your office."

"Well, thanks again, Jill. I most definitely owe you one."

***

I was concerned about the twins and Cuppy C. The downturn in trade resulting from the ice maidens' antics had hit their business hard. I expected them to be down in the dumps about the situation, but when I magicked myself over there, they were obviously in good humour.

"Hi, Jill." Amber was all smiles.

"Hey there, Jill." Pearl came skipping over.

"I didn't think you two would be this chipper. Have you won the lottery?"

"We don't have a lottery here in Candlefield," Pearl said. "I think we should, but the Combined Sup Council always vetoes the idea."

"They veto everything that's fun." Amber sighed.

"So, if it isn't the lottery, why are you both so happy?"

"We've had a great idea!" Pearl was bursting with excitement.

"This is without doubt the best idea we've ever come up with." Amber agreed.

Call me cynical, but whenever the twins had a good idea, I always feared the worst. "What kind of idea?"

"We were going to put an advert in The Candle to tell everyone that our prices were back to normal, but we weren't sure that people would even notice it. We needed something much more exciting and eye-catching to advertise. Something that was guaranteed to bring the customers back in droves."

"What have you dreamed up this time?"

"Actually, it wasn't our idea. Perry and Simon came up with it."

"Who are they?"

"Our new tenants." Pearl gestured upstairs.

"You mean the Sweaty Boys?"

"Adrenaline! They suggested that they could put on a show right here in Cuppy C."

"They? You mean their dance troupe?"

"Yeah! It's a brilliant idea, don't you think?"

There were many words to describe what I thought of the idea, but 'brilliant' wasn't even on the list.

"There isn't room in here for them to do their act."

"That's what we thought," Pearl said. "But Perry said that they often do private functions in small rooms."

"I'm really not sure their act is suitable for Cuppy C. It's not exactly family friendly, is it? Don't you think it might be too raunchy?"

"Perry says that they have a family friendly version of their routine where they don't take off any of their clothes. They just dance."

"I see. I still think your original idea of just informing

people that the prices are back to normal is the way to go."

"No way." Amber shook her head. "This will have way more impact."

"Yeah!" Pearl said. "People will be talking about this for ages."

I didn't doubt that for one moment.

***

Back in Washbridge, I went to the office to check if there was anything which required my attention. There had been no phone calls, and Winky was fast asleep, so I decided to finish early. After all, I had important business to attend to.

As soon as I got home, I took out the Biscuit Barrel Monthly magazine which Winky had so kindly acquired for me. I hadn't wanted to complete the competition in the office because there were too many distractions. Likewise, I didn't want to attempt it while Jack was there because I needed to give it my undivided attention. I had a couple of hours until the deadline for online entries.

It was one of those competitions which I hated. The ones where you have to finish off a sentence. In this case, it was: 'Custard creams are the king of biscuits because...'

There were so many reasons I could have given, but I had to find just the right one. Something that would resonate with the publishers of Biscuit Barrel Monthly. An hour later, and I was still struggling to come up with the right words. And then, it came to me—the perfect wording: 'Custard creams are the king of biscuits because they make me feel as though I can do magic.'

I logged onto the magazine's website, entered the unique code from my copy of the magazine, and then submitted my entry. The winner would be notified by post two days later. I could almost taste those custard creams. Just think how much money I'd save over the course of a year.

Jack arrived home about an hour later. He looked fed up.

"What's wrong?"

"Nothing. It's just the same old politics. It gets me down sometimes. How about you? How was your day?"

"Okay. Kathy was back at work today."

"How's she doing?"

"I'm not really sure. I don't think she should be back at work yet, but she's had enough of just hanging around the house."

"Has she heard any more from Riley about the Lucinda affair?"

"I don't think so. Do you think you could find out what's going on with it?"

"I'll ask around tomorrow, and see what I can find out."

***

I couldn't see the end of the corridor. It seemed to stretch out in front of me for miles and miles. There were no doors on either side. I picked up my pace, and began to run even faster, but didn't seem to make any headway. Then at last, I came to a staircase. It was dark below, so I had to tread carefully. When I reached the bottom, a light illuminated the room. In front of me was a door. Instinctively, I knew there was something dangerous lurking inside; something evil. But I had no choice—I had to find out what was on the other side. I turned the handle, opened the door, and stepped inside.

"I've been waiting so long for you," the man said.

The last time I'd seen this red-haired, red-bearded man, he'd been lying dead in a cupboard near to my office.

"Jill! Wake up!"

I opened my eyes to find Jack looking down at me, obviously concerned.

"Are you okay?"

"I think so."

"You were having that nightmare again, weren't you?"

"Yeah."

"What was it about?"

"I wish I knew."

Chapter 22

The next morning, I'd no sooner walked into my office than my mother appeared.

"Have you spoken to him, yet?"

"Spoken to who?"

She gave a deep sigh. "I asked if you'd speak to your father about the house. Did you forget?"

Totally.

"No, of course not. I've been really busy."

"Too busy to find five minutes?"

"Sorry. I'll do it today."

"Promise?"

"I promise."

After she'd disappeared, Winky came out from under the sofa. "I don't know why you put yourself at everyone's beck and call. If it isn't your crazy grandmother or your sister, then it's some ghost or other. You should put yourself first for a change."

"You're right, Winky. I'm always putting myself out for other people. It's time I looked after number one."

"Good for you. Now get me some salmon, would you?"

After I'd fed Winky, I decided I might as well speak to my father, because if I didn't, I'd probably forget again.

"Dad! Are you there, Dad?"

I didn't sense the chill which usually preceded his appearance, so I tried again. "Dad! Are you there?"

The temperature in the room dropped. He must have heard my call.

"Hello, Jill," Blodwyn said. "Your dad is on the roof, replacing a tile. He asked me to see what you wanted."

"This is a little awkward. I had a visit from my mother.

She's not very happy about you and my father moving into the same street as her."

"To tell you the truth, neither am I. I told your dad that I didn't think it was a good idea, but he said we wouldn't find a better property for the money anywhere else."

"Is property expensive in Ghost Town, then?"

"Incredibly. So many people are choosing to stop off in Ghost Town these days that demand outstrips supply. I can tell your dad what you said, if you like?"

"No, don't bother. I think this is something that Mum and Dad will have to sort out between themselves. Anyway, it was nice to see you again, Blodwyn. How are you and my dad getting along?"

"Like a house on fire. Your father has a lot of stamina for a man of his age, if you know what I mean." She grinned.

Way too much information.

***

My initial impression of Michael Gray had been that he wasn't the kind of man who was capable of murder, but the fact that the poison used to kill Lucinda was found only in commercial laboratories was a strong pointer in his direction. The police must also have made that connection, but still appeared to have eliminated him from their enquiries. Still, I owed it to myself to have another chat with Mr Gray, to see if I could shake anything out of him. This time though, I wanted to do it without the use of magic. I was concerned that the Michael Gray I'd seen the first time might not be the real Michael Gray. Maybe he'd been so shocked by the magic that he'd come across as timider than he would normally have been.

Getting to see him wasn't going to be easy, but I was determined that before the day was out, he and I would have had a conversation.

I turned up at the reception of Gemini Chemicals late morning.

"I'd like to see Mr Michael Gray, please."

"Do you have an appointment?"

"No."

"What's your name, please?"

"Jill Gooder. He won't know me, but if you could tell him it's in connection with his ex-wife."

The receptionist made a call, and I could tell from the half of the conversation that I could hear, that I wasn't going to get an audience with Gray. While she was talking to him, I looked again at the large framed photograph, which dated back to when the business had first opened, ten years earlier. This time, I spotted a familiar face. The man standing next to Michael Gray had long hair. That same man looked very different today.

"I'm very sorry," the receptionist said. "Mr Gray can't see you."

"That's okay. I don't need to speak to him now."

I had a hunch, but before I could act upon it, I'd need to speak to Donna Proudlove again. This time, she took my call first time, and agreed to meet me in reception at Wool TV.

"Donna, thanks for seeing me."

"That's okay. I just hope you don't still suspect me of killing Lucinda?"

"No. I'm now sure you didn't have anything to do with

it. I need a couple of favours from you. I'd like to take another look at the CCTV, but this time for the morning of the day that Lucinda was murdered."

"Sure. I'll take you there now."

I followed her through to the security office where she set me up to view the tape for the day of the murder.

"You can leave me here, Donna. It might take me a while to go through this."

"You said there were two things you needed from me?"

"Yeah. I wanted to ask you a question. You mentioned that Lucinda had got rid of a photographer."

"That's right. I still can't remember his name. I just remember that he was bald."

"Could it have been Shane Fairweather?"

"Yeah. That was him. She kicked him out about two months ago."

I began to work my way through the tape. Twenty-five minutes in, I found what I was hoping for.

***

I made my way to Washbridge Studios where I tried the door, and rang the buzzer several times, but there was no reply. I could have used the 'power' spell to force my way inside, but that seemed a little heavy-handed, and I preferred not to leave any evidence that I'd been there in case my suspicions proved to be unfounded.

Underneath the window was a small aluminium grille. I checked to make sure there was no one around, and then shrank myself so I could climb through it. Once inside, I reversed the 'shrink' spell, and made my way through to the studio where I'd watched Callum's photo shoot. There were two doors off the studio. The first one was a small dressing room. The second was obviously Shane Fairweather's office which was something of a shambles. There were papers strewn all over his desk. I took a seat and began to sift through them. In only a matter of minutes, I'd established that his business was in a whole heap of trouble. His bank statements showed that he was overdrawn. There were several letters from suppliers demanding payment for overdue bills. Also on his desk was a folder marked 'sales.' Inside it were a number of printouts which showed his sales figures had plummeted dramatically about two months earlier. That would coincide with the time that Lucinda had ended his contract with Wool TV. It was quite apparent that Shane Fairweather's business had depended heavily on the assignments he'd undertaken for Wool TV. Losing that account had had a devastating effect on his business.

At that precise moment, I heard the door open.

"Hello, Mr Fairweather."

"What are you doing in here? Who let you in?"

"The door was open," I lied.

"No it wasn't! I locked it. Why are you here?"

"Did you really think you could get away with Lucinda's murder?"

The shock registered on his face, but he quickly recovered. "What are you talking about?"

"You were caught on CCTV going into the Wool TV studios on the morning Lucinda died."

"Is that it?" He sneered. "Is that the basis of your accusation? I went in there to pick up some of my things. I was only in there for a few minutes."

"Long enough to inject poison into the bottle of water,

and then plant the syringe in Kathy's desk. You knew which bottle Lucinda would be drinking from, didn't you? Isn't it true that she always drank the same Blackstone Spa water?"

"How would I know?"

"You worked with her often enough, didn't you? In fact, according to your own sales figures, your assignments at Wool TV made up almost fifty percent of your income. It must have come as a bitter blow when Lucinda decided to cancel your contract."

"None of this proves anything."

"You're right, of course. Taken individually, none of this adds up to very much. But when you put it all together, it makes a fairly strong case against you. The mounting debts and overdraft—you were under a lot of pressure to recover the lost income. Is that what you and she were arguing about in this very studio? Had you asked her for a second chance? From what I hear, Lucinda wasn't the kind of person to change her mind. When she refused to budge, you were left with no choice, were you? You had to find some way to recover that contract, didn't you? What better way to do that than to get rid of Lucinda. Her successor may have been more receptive to continuing the relationship you'd had with the studio."

"Anyone could have poisoned her. She'd made a lot of enemies."

"That's true, but not many of them would have had access to the particular poison which you used to kill her. Only someone who had connections to commercial laboratories would have been able to get hold of that. And of course, in your previous career at Gemini Chemicals, you would have established just such connections. I've seen the company photograph from ten years ago. You had a lot more hair in those days, didn't you?"

The colour drained from his face, but he wasn't ready to admit his guilt yet.

"Get out of here! Now!"

"I'm going, but I should tell you that I will be handing over all of this information to the police."

I turned to walk away, but heard his footsteps coming up behind me. I spun around just in time to grab his arm. He'd been about to hit me over the back of the head with a paperweight. After casting the 'power' spell, I easily disarmed him, and then used the 'tie-up' spell to bind his hands and feet.

Thirty minutes after my phone call to the police, Leo Riley and three uniformed officers arrived at Washbridge Studios.

"Arrest her!" Fairweather demanded. "And untie me!"

"What's going on here, Gooder? This had better be good."

"This man poisoned Lucinda Gray."

"Don't listen to her!" Fairweather shouted. "She's a lunatic."

"I think you'd both better come down to the station." Riley turned to one of the officers. "Untie this man."

Back at the station, Fairweather and I were both booked in, and then placed in separate holding cells. An hour later, I was taken out of the cell, and led to one of the interview rooms where Riley was waiting for me.

"Okay, what's the story?" he demanded.

"Fairweather used to do a lot of work for Wool TV. In fact, it made up almost half of his total turnover. But it seems he got on the wrong side of Lucinda Gray, who cancelled his contract. The man was in desperate financial straits, and needed to regain the business from Wool TV. He figured the only way to do that was to get rid of Lucinda Gray. My guess is that he saw the news reports of the first poisoning, and decided to kill Lucinda in a similar way, in the hope that the murders would be linked. His big mistake was using a completely different poison, but of course he had no way of knowing what the first murderer had used. Shane Fairweather used to work at Gemini Chemicals before opting for a career change. He still had contacts in the industry, and would have been able to get his hands on the quick-acting poison, which he injected into Lucinda Gray's water bottle. If you check the CCTV, you'll find that he paid a brief visit to the studio on the morning of the murder."

"We're already aware of Fairweather's visit to the studio. We've seen the CCTV. But even with that there's precious little proof that he murdered Lucinda Grey. And none of this excuses your attacking him and tying him up. What's to stop me charging you with assault, at the very least?"

"That was self-defence. He came at me with a paperweight."

"It would never have happened if you'd kept your nose out, as I asked you to."

The questioning dragged on for another hour before he finally released me. He wouldn't confirm whether Fairweather had also been released.

***

"Where have you been?" Jack said when I eventually arrived home.

"At Washbridge police station, talking to my old friend, Leo Riley."

Jack shook his head. "What have you done this time?"

"Solved another case for him."

"Which one?"

"Lucinda Gray's murder. A photographer named Shane Fairweather killed her."

"Do you have proof?"

"Only circumstantial."

"What did Riley have to say?"

"I thought for a while he was going to charge *me* with assault."

"Why? What had you done?"

"Fairweather came at me with a paperweight, so I had to restrain him. It was self defence."

"Jill! How many times have I told you not to put yourself at risk?"

"I was never in any danger. I can handle people like Fairweather."

"Are they going to charge him?

"I've no idea. Riley wouldn't tell me."

"Have you let Kathy know?"

"Not yet. I don't want to say anything until I know for sure whether he's been charged. I won't get the chance tomorrow, anyway."

"Why? What are you up to tomorrow?"

"It's that stupid Woolcon."

"Oh yeah." He laughed. "I'd forgotten about that."

"I wish I could forget about it. I don't know what possessed me to agree to go."

"Do I get to see it?"

"See what?"

"Your costume. You are going to wear one, aren't you?"

"No, I'm not. I told Mrs V and Jules I'd only go on condition that I didn't have to wear a silly costume."

"That's a shame. I think you'd look sexy dressed as a ball of wool."

"Sometimes, I worry about you, Jack."

Chapter 23

"Bill, bill, another bill." Jack had just picked up the post from the doormat. "This one is for you." He handed me a letter.

The name printed on the back of the envelope was 'Biscuit Periodicals.' Could it be? I tore it open, and quickly read the letter.

"Yes! Yes!" I did a happy dance around the kitchen.

"Are you feeling okay, Jill?"

"I've never felt better." I held up the sheet of paper. "Look, I've won."

"Won what?"

"This!" I passed it to him while I went back to my happy dance.

"You didn't tell me that you'd entered this competition."

"I didn't think I had a chance of winning."

"Have you seen this? You have to go down there tomorrow to collect your prize. They're based in London."

"That's okay. It'll be worth it to get a year's supply of custard creams."

"How's that going to work, anyway? Will you have to carry them all back with you?"

I rolled my eyes. "How did you ever get to be a detective? They're not going to give me boxes full of custard creams to bring back with me. They'll probably give me vouchers."

"Oh yeah." He laughed. "Of course."

Long after Jack had left for work, I kept reading and rereading the letter. I'd actually won. Me! I'd never won a competition before in my life. I wanted to share my good news, so I called Kathy.

"I have exciting news. You'll never guess what!"

"You're pregnant?"

"No, I'm not pregnant. I've won a competition! It's the best prize ever."

"What is it? A new car?"

"A year's supply of custard creams."

"Is that all?" She couldn't have sounded any less impressed.

"I have to go down to London tomorrow to collect the prize."

"Are they paying for you to go down there?"

"No. I have to pay my travel expenses, but it'll be well worth it to get one year's free supply of custard creams."

"Congratulations, I guess. It's just a pity that you couldn't have a mixture of biscuits."

"Why would I want that?"

***

Mrs V and Jules were waiting for me outside our office building. They were both carrying huge bags—no doubt their costumes.

"Hey, you two, I have fantastic news."

"You've decided to wear a costume?" Jules said.

"No. I told you. I'm not wearing a stupid costume."

"You're pregnant?" Mrs V said.

"No! Why does everyone jump to that conclusion? I've won a competition, and you'll never guess what the prize is."

"A world cruise?" Mrs V suggested.

"No."

"A yacht?" Jules said.

"No. A year's supply of custard creams."

"Oh. What was the first prize?"

"That *was* first prize."

"I'm very pleased for you, dear." Just like Kathy, Mrs V didn't sound very impressed. "It's a pity you can only have custard creams though, isn't it? A mixture would have been better."

What was wrong with people?

Wow! Who knew that Woolcon was such a big deal?

When we arrived at the exhibition centre, I discovered that Woolcon occupied two of the largest halls. It took me over twenty minutes just to park, and then we had another ten-minute walk to get to the main entrance.

Every conversation I overheard was related to yarn in one way or another. Mrs V and Jules were like two young kids on Christmas morning. First stop was the cloakroom where the attendees could leave their bags. Some people were already wearing costumes, but the majority, like Mrs V and Jules, planned to put theirs on later in time for the masquerade.

"Where shall we go first?" Jules was looking around excitedly.

"How about we get some food?" I suggested.

"We didn't come all this way just to eat." Mrs V slapped me down. "There's far too much to see to waste time sitting in a restaurant. You'll have to grab a sandwich as we go."

That had told me.

"Let's go see the exhibitors." Jules pointed to the far side of the hall.

Mrs V and Jules set off apace; I followed them. The exhibitors' section of the hall was absolutely buzzing. There was aisle after aisle of stands of all shapes and sizes, ranging from the multinational yarn companies to the small mom-and-pop operations.

"We have to grab all the free samples we can get," Jules said.

"Will there be any free custard creams?"

They either didn't hear me, or more likely, ignored me. They were too busy collecting samples of wool, and other yarn merchandise.

"You two are wearing me out," I complained after an hour. "I need a sit-down. Can we go and get a cup of tea?"

"We've barely started." Mrs V was clearly losing patience with me. "Why don't you go and get a drink, and meet us back here in thirty minutes?"

"Okay." I made my escape before she had the chance to change her mind.

On my way to the restaurant, I noticed a particularly large crowd around one of the small stands located on the outer edge of the hall. I was curious as to what could attract so many people, so decided to check it out en route to the restaurant. As I got closer, I could see numerous man-sized balls of wool handing out chocolates, cakes and drinks. Maybe, I could save myself the cost of a visit to the restaurant. After all, the prices in these places were always exorbitant.

I spotted a particularly delicious looking strawberry cupcake on the tray being carried by the red ball of wool. Result!

I reached out to grab it, but someone slapped my hand away.

"You can buy your own, young lady!"

"Grandma? What are you doing here? You didn't tell me you were going to visit Woolcon."

"I'm not a visitor. I'm an exhibitor." She grabbed my arm and led me through the crowd of people who were milling around the stand. "See!"

The stand belonged to Ever A Wool Moment, and it was doing a brisk trade in Everlasting Wool, One-Size Needles, and cupcakes.

"The stand seems to be doing well, Grandma."

"Of course it is. No one has products to match these. Who have you come here with, anyway?"

"Mrs V and Jules."

"If I'd realised that you three were coming, I needn't have bothered hiring the promotional staff to dress as balls of wool."

Fortunately, just at that moment, a couple of elderly women asked if they could have a selfie with Grandma. That was my chance to make a break for it.

"I'd better be getting back." I started to edge away. "Mrs V and Jules will be wondering where I am."

As I made my escape, I grabbed the strawberry cupcake, and then found a quiet spot to rest up for a while.

"Did you know your grandmother is here?" Mrs V said when the three of us met up later.

"Yeah, I've seen her. She never mentioned that she'd be attending."

"She tried to get me and Jules to help her on her stand."

"I'm surprised you managed to get away."

"I didn't come all this way just to help your grandmother, and besides we want to see the celebrities."

"Which celebrities?"

"There are lots of them, Jill." Jules pointed to her programme. "They're upstairs in the Blue Suite."

I had no burning desire to meet the yarn celebrities, but I was worried that if I stayed behind, Grandma might come looking for me.

Tables lined all four walls of the Blue Suite. Behind each of them sat the so-called celebrities. There were queues at every table. Autographs were being signed, and photographs being taken everywhere I looked.

"Over there!" Mrs V pointed. "It's Kirsten Bracken. I must get her autograph."

"Me too." Jules hurried after her.

I followed somewhat less enthusiastically.

"Who exactly is Kirsten Bracken?" I whispered just in case I was overheard by the many adoring fans who were waiting to see this superstar of the yarn industry.

"Who is she?" Mrs V gave me a look of disgust.

"How can you not know?" Jules shook her head.

"She invented the triple-loop stitch," Mrs V said, as though I was some kind of idiot.

We were in the queue for the best part of thirty minutes just so Mrs V and Jules could pose for a selfie with Kirsten Triple-loop.

"Would you like a photo too?" Kirsten turned to me.

"No thanks. I'm good."

Kirsten Bracken wasn't the only celebrity that Mrs V and Jules wanted to see. By the time we'd queued for them all, I'd almost lost the will to live.

"Is it time to go home yet?" I was dead on my feet.

"It's the masquerade now!" Jules could barely contain her excitement.

The two of them dragged me to the cloakroom to collect their bags.

"There's something we need to ask you, Jill," Mrs V said.

"Please say yes, Jill," Jules pleaded.

"What?" I didn't like the sound of this. Not one tiny little bit.

"There's a competition we want to enter in the masquerade. The first prize is a year's supply of Crownleaf wool," Mrs V said. "Crownleaf is the best wool in the world – they have shades that no one else does."

"It's the absolute best," Jules gushed.

"So what is this favour that you need from me?"

"The competition is for the best costumed trio. That's a knitting needle, a ball of wool, and a crochet hook."

"I don't see how you can enter it, then. You're one man short."

"Not necessarily." Mrs V took her costume out of her bag, and then brought out another one.

Oh no!

"I told you that I wasn't going to wear a silly costume."

"Please, Jill!" Jules gave me her sad face. "We can't even enter unless you take part too."

"Just think how good it will be for office morale," Mrs V said.

"Please, Jill." Jules wasn't letting up. "I'll work twice as hard from now on."

These two had had this planned all along; they must have known about the competition for weeks. But how could I say no. It would have been like kicking a pair of sad puppies.

"Okay. Give me the stupid costume."

And so it was that thirty minutes later, I was parading around the hall dressed as a crochet hook. I just thanked my lucky stars that Jack, Kathy or anyone else who knew me, couldn't see me now.

The masquerade went on for an hour short of eternity. It was so hot inside that stupid costume that by the time I was able to peel it off, I must have lost several pounds. It wouldn't have been quite so bad if we had won, but we didn't even place in the top three.

"Your heart wasn't in it," Mrs V blamed me for our failure.

"I did my best. I don't have a lot of experience of being a crochet hook."

By the time I'd dropped both Mrs V and Jules off at their homes, and made my way back to Smallwash, it was almost midnight, and I was absolutely bushed. Jack didn't even stir when I climbed into bed beside him.

***

I'd been running along the corridors for ages, but seemingly getting nowhere. At last, I came to a staircase. When I reached the bottom, I saw a door in front of me. I had to find out what was on the other side, regardless of the danger. I turned the handle.

"Where have you been?" the man said.

It was the red-haired, red-bearded man again.

I sat up in bed. Jack was still fast asleep. He must have become accustomed to my nightmares—hardly surprising considering how often I was having them.

This couldn't go on.

Chapter 24

The recurring nightmare was beginning to get to me. It was getting to the point where I didn't want to go to sleep for fear of having that same nightmare again. Then I remembered what Daze had told me about the pupil at CASS who had found the dream-stone. The idea that there was another world where dreams were a reality was hard to accept, but then as Daze had quite rightly pointed out, I would have felt the same about Candlefield not so very long ago.

If it was true, and this guy could actually travel to the dream world, then maybe he could help me to make sense of the recurring nightmare. Daze had told me his name was Edward Hedgelog. Surely there couldn't be more than one wizard in Candlefield with that name. I decided to start with Candlefield Pages. If I drew a blank there, I'd have to pay a visit to Candlefield library.

I flicked through the 'alphabetical by name' section, and found one business listed under that name: Hedgelog Bicycle Repairs. It seemed unlikely that a wizard who had been picked out to attend CASS, and who had found one of only seven dream-stones, would now be in the bicycle repair business. But, as the shop was on my way to the library anyway, I decided to call in—just in case.

Hedgelog Bicycle Repairs was in a side street next door to a quaint little coffee shop called Bean A While. The window of the bike shop looked as though it hadn't been cleaned for several months. Inside, it was poky and very untidy.

I heard footsteps coming from somewhere in the back.

"Yes?" The man was wearing a green smock. He had

dark brown hair, but a pure white moustache. "Aren't you Jill Gooder?"

His question caught me off-guard. "Yes, I am. How did you know?"

"It's such an honour to meet you. I've been following your progress ever since you took part in the Levels Competition. I'm a big fan of the Levels, and I was very impressed by your debut. I was sorry to see that you didn't enter last year. Will you be taking part this year?"

"Yes, I think so."

"If you do, my money will be on you to win." He reached under the counter and brought out a small booklet. On closer examination, I realised it was a programme for the Levels Competition in which I had competed.

"Could I have your autograph?" He handed me the programme and a pen.

"Of course." I scribbled my signature on the front cover. Apparently, Kathy wasn't the only celebrity in the family.

"Thank you so much." He held the programme to his heart. It was all a little embarrassing. Who would have thought I had a fanboy?

"You're not by any chance the Edward Hedgelog who went to CASS?"

"Yes. How did you know?"

"Daze told me. She was in the same year as you."

"Daze?" He looked a little puzzled. "I don't know anyone by that name."

"You might have known her by the name: Daisy Flowers."

"Oh yes. I remember Daisy, and come to think of it she didn't like anyone calling her that, but I'd totally forgotten her nickname. What is she doing now?"

"She's a Rogue Retriever."

"That makes sense. She was always the sporty type, and something of a tomboy." He glanced through the window. "Do you have a bicycle in need of repair?"

"No. That's not why I'm here. Daze told me that while at CASS you found one of the dream-stones."

"Oh, that." His face fell.

"Is it true?"

"Yes, but I very much wish I hadn't."

"Why is that?"

"Delving into the dream world is not what I wanted to do with my life. I've always had a passion for bicycles, and in particular repairing them. That's why I opened this place. I've tried to put the dream-stone thing behind me."

"Not entirely, I hope? I was hoping that I could persuade you to help me with a recurring nightmare which I've been having."

"I'd really rather not get involved."

"How about if I were to promise you a signed photograph of me collecting the Levels trophy if I were to win it this year?"

His face lit up. "Would you?"

"Yes, but only if you help me to unravel my nightmare."

"Deal!"

"Great! What do you need me to do?"

"I have to be in the room with you when you fall asleep."

"Oh? That's going to be difficult. I live with a human. I'm not sure—"

"You can come to my house. Provided that you're able

to fall asleep in the chair, I should be able to access your nightmare."

"Okay. That works for me. Can you let me have your address?"

"Sure." He scribbled it on a scrap of paper and handed it to me. "When did you want to do it?"

"Tonight, if that's possible. I want to get to the bottom of this."

"Tonight it is."

***

Even though I knew the twins' latest escapade was going to be a disaster, I had to check it out for myself.

I could barely get through the door at Cuppy C; I'd never seen the place so packed. All the seats were taken, and there was very little standing room. Noticeably, there wasn't a man to be seen in the place. The twins had closed the cake counter, and brought in two extra assistants. It took me ten minutes just to squeeze my way through to the tea room counter.

"What did we tell you?" Pearl said. "Didn't we say this was a great idea?"

"Looks like you were right," I conceded. "Can I get a latte and a blueberry muffin, please?"

"We'll have to start turning them away soon." Amber passed me a slice of carrot cake.

"What's this?"

"It's all we've got left. All the other cakes have gone. We should have brought in more stock."

There was no way that I was going to get a seat, so I joined the twins behind the counter.

"We want the Adrenaline Boys!" The crowd began to chant. "We want the Adrenaline Boys!"

"What time are they meant to come on?" I asked.

"In five minutes." Pearl gave someone the last piece of carrot cake.

The audience continued to shout for the show to begin.

Suddenly, the lights dimmed, and a single spotlight lit the wall closest to the stairs. The crowd fell silent, and the sense of anticipation was palpable. Then the music began, and the Adrenaline Boys appeared. All four of them were dressed in tight leather trousers and black t-shirts. Jethro was standing on the far left. A guy with long blond hair stepped forward.

"We are the Adrenaline Boys."

With that, they went into their first routine. Just as the twins had promised, it was far less raunchy than the show I'd seen with Mad, but that didn't stop the audience getting more and more excited. After a few minutes, most of the crowd were on their feet, dancing—and edging closer and closer to the Adrenaline Boys.

"Get your shirt off!" Someone shouted.

"Show us your chest!" Another voice.

Soon, the music was drowned out by calls for the boys to shed their clothes.

"We have to stop this." Pearl looked worried. "If they strip, the authorities will close down Cuppy C."

"How can we stop them?" Amber said. "If we pull them off stage now, this crowd will lynch us."

"We have to do something." Pearl sounded desperate.

The twins were right. The situation was getting out of hand, but how were they going to get the boys out of there? Then, I had an idea.

Water began to pour down on the audience who rushed to the door to escape the deluge. Pearl took that opportunity to lead the Adrenaline Boys back upstairs.

"Lock the door," I yelled at Amber, as soon as I'd reversed the 'rain' spell.

An hour later, we were still mopping up the water when the Adrenaline Boys came back downstairs.

"Thank goodness you got that lot out of here," Jethro said. "That crowd was wild. Much worse than our usual audience."

***

That evening, I found Edward Hedgelog's house without much difficulty. The pretty little thatched cottage with the beautiful front garden wasn't at all what I'd expected. The only clue that he lived there was the name on the plaque: 'On yer bike.'

"Jill, do come in. Did you find me okay?" He was wearing a smoking jacket and cravat—quite the contrast to the green smock he'd sported in the bicycle shop.

"Yes. No problem at all. You have a beautiful garden."

"Thank you. After bicycles, gardening is my next biggest passion."

He led me through to the lounge at the rear of the house. It had large French windows which looked out onto an equally impressive back garden.

"Take a seat there please, Jill." He pointed to a floral design rocking chair.

I did as he asked, and he took a seat opposite me in a red leather armchair.

"So, how exactly does this work?"

"It's quite simple really. Once you're asleep, I'll use the dream-stone to enter your dream. Once there, I should be able to find out exactly what's causing you to have the nightmares. Do you think you'll be able to get to sleep?"

"That shouldn't be a problem." I reached into my handbag.

"Sleeping pills?"

"No. I have something much better than that. This is guaranteed to send me to sleep."

"What is that you're reading?"

"It's a movie newsletter, which is written by an ex-neighbour of mine."

There was corridor after corridor. No matter how hard I tried, I couldn't go any faster. After what felt like forever, I came to a staircase. I took the stairs two at a time. Once at the bottom, I found myself facing a door. I could sense there was danger behind it, but I had to find out what was inside. I turned the handle.

"Jill! Wake up, Jill!"

Someone was shaking me, and I could hear a voice in the distance.

"Jill, wake up!"

I was back in the rocking chair, facing the garden.

"Are you okay?" Edward Hedgelog was standing next to me.

"I'm fine. Did it work?"

"Yes. Well, kind of."

"What do you mean? Were you able to get into my dream or not?"

"Yes, that wasn't a problem. I'm just not sure I understand what I learned there."

"Tell me what you found out."

"Someone is trying to get a message to you. He's trying to warn you of danger that you'll be facing very shortly."

"Who is *he*?"

"He didn't tell me his name."

"Did he have red hair and a red beard?"

"Yes. Do you know him?"

"No. I've seen him, but I have no idea who he is."

"That's very strange." Edward sat back down in the armchair. "He said that you had to remember the promise that you and he had made, and that you must act quickly because others were determined to stop you."

"None of this makes a lick of sense." I sighed. "Will I still get the nightmares?"

"I don't think so. Not now he's managed to deliver his message to you via me."

"Thank you for your help, Edward," I said as he showed me to the door.

"I'm sorry I couldn't find any more information. You won't forget the signed photograph when you win the Levels, will you?"

"*If* I win."

"You'll win. There's no doubt about that."

I felt deflated. I wasn't sure what I'd expected, but I was even more confused now than I'd been before. When the red-haired, red-bearded man had turned up at my door in Smallwash, I'd assumed he was some kind of nutcase. It seemed I was right because he was now claiming that he and I had made a promise together. I know my memory can be bad at times, but I'm pretty sure I would have remembered that.

I'd just have to hope that this would at least put an end to the nightmares.

Chapter 25

Yay! I'd had two consecutive nights without nightmares! Maybe the visit to Edward Hedgelog had been worth it after all.

The big day had arrived. Today was the day I went to London to collect my competition prize. I wasn't due to get there until mid-afternoon, so had plenty of time before I had to catch the train. I planned to call into the office first, to check if I had any mail or telephone messages. I needn't have bothered. The only mail was a bill, and the only message on the answerphone was someone wanting a quotation for a new garage door. Huh?

"Nice of you to turn in," Winky said. "Where have you been hiding?"

"I've been catching up with some jobs in the house."

"So, you haven't been walking around dressed as a crochet hook, then?"

How did he know? "I don't know what you're talking about." When in doubt: deny, deny, deny.

"This isn't you with the old bag lady and Jules, then?"

He held up his smartphone to show me a series of images taken at Woolcon. And there I was, dressed as a crochet hook, standing next to a ball of wool and a knitting needle.

"That's not me!"

He grinned.

"I'm telling you, that's not me. It must be someone else. Anyway, I can't stay here and argue with you. I'm going to London today."

"Can I come?"

"No. You can stay here and practise your deportment."

I still had time to kill, so I decided to call in on Kathy and Peter.

"Jill?" Kathy looked stressed when she answered the door. "Aren't you supposed to be in London today?"

"Yeah, but my train isn't until later. I thought I'd check on how you were doing. I'm not interrupting anything, am I?"

"No. It's just Pete—he's doing my head in."

I followed her into the lounge. Peter was sitting on the sofa.

"Hi, Jill." He looked cheesed off.

"I feel like I've walked in on something."

"Tell her, Pete."

"There's nothing to tell."

"I'll tell her, then," Kathy said. "That neighbour of yours is poaching Pete's customers. She's signed up four of them already."

"Megan?"

"Who else? Megan and her hot pants. I told him to have a word with her, and warn her off, but he won't."

"It's called competition, Kathy," Peter said. "I don't have a divine right to keep any customer."

"Yeah, but how are you meant to compete with her skimpy top and short shorts?"

"Maybe I could start wearing hot pants?" He laughed.

Kathy didn't.

"I'm glad you think it's funny because I don't." Kathy fixed him with her gaze. "Megan and her hot pants are stealing food out of our kids' mouths."

"You're being melodramatic as usual," Peter said. "Tell her, Jill!"

"Hey! Leave me out of this."

"You should have a word with Megan, Jill," Kathy said. "She's your neighbour."

"What exactly am I meant to say to her? Don't flash your hot pants at Peter's customers?"

"Yeah, something like that."

Just then, Lizzie came out of her bedroom, and rushed over to me. She was much happier than she'd been the last time I'd seen her.

"Hiya, Auntie Jill."

"Hi. You look very happy today?"

"Katie is my best friend again."

"That's good news. I'm really pleased for you."

"Joe Bear isn't. He's really sad because he can't be my best friend anymore. He keeps asking me why I've found a new best friend."

"He's only a toy," Kathy said. "He can't be sad."

"But he is, Mummy. He's been crying."

"Now you're being silly, Lizzie."

"No, I'm not!"

It was time for me to step in. I knew that Lizzie was telling the truth about Joe Bear.

Why don't I go and talk to Joe Bear, Lizzie?"

"Would you, Auntie Jill?"

"Sure. You stay here with Mummy and Daddy, and I'll go and have a word with him."

I left Lizzie, Kathy and Peter in the lounge while I went to Lizzie's bedroom. Joe Bear was on her bed. After closing the door behind me, I reversed the 'enchantment' spell. Joe Bear's work was done; Lizzie now had a real life BFF.

***

Normally, when I travelled by train, I went standard class, but I'd decided that such an auspicious occasion deserved something better. The price of the first-class ticket had brought tears to my eyes, but given that I would be getting a year's supply of custard creams it seemed worth it.

"Good morning," I said to the man in the pinstriped suit seated opposite me.

He looked at me over his newspaper. "Good morning."

"Are you going to London on business?"

"Yes."

"Do you go down there often?"

"Most days."

"I'm going to collect a prize."

"Really?"

He was pretending to be uninterested, but I knew he was dying to know what I'd won.

"I won the competition in Biscuit Barrel Monthly magazine; a year's supply of custard creams."

"Custard what?"

Was this guy for real? "Creams. You know, custard creams."

"That must be very exciting for you." He was trying to hide it, but I could tell he was green with envy.

The offices of Biscuit Periodicals were some distance from the train station. I could have taken the tube, but I figured it would be crowded. The letter had mentioned that they'd be taking photographs, so I wanted to arrive there looking my best.

I hailed a taxi.

"I'm going to pick up a prize." I gave the driver the address.

"Really, love? What kind of prize?"

"A year's supply of custard creams."

"They're the Mrs's favourite. Me, I prefer Garibaldi."

That was wrong on so many levels, but I didn't feel I should comment.

Fifteen minutes later, the taxi dropped me right outside the offices of Biscuit Periodicals. The fare was a little more than I'd expected, but I still gave the driver a tip.

"Good morning," the bubbly young woman behind reception greeted me.

"Morning. My name is Jill Gooder. I'm here to collect a competition prize."

"Biscuit Barrel Monthly?"

"That's the one."

"Take a seat over there please. Someone will collect you in a few minutes."

There was a selection of magazines in the waiting area—all of which were biscuit related. I'd just started to flip through Biscuit Digest Quarterly when the door to the right of the reception desk opened, and a young man with streaked blond hair emerged. He was wearing a silver-grey, double-breasted suit.

"Jill?"

I stood up. "That's me."

"Jason Finger. Pleased to meet you. Please come with me. We'll be making the presentation in the Ginger Suite."

We took the lift to the third floor. The Ginger Suite was directly opposite the lift doors.

"This way."

Waiting for us inside was a woman who greeted me

with a broad smile. Standing next to her, was a photographer.

"You must be Jill," the woman said. "I'm Amanda Short. Congratulations on your win."

"Thank you. This is the first competition I've ever won."

"Jimmy is going to take a photograph of the presentation. It will appear in next month's issue, if that's okay with you?"

"Sure. That's great."

"Okay then. On behalf of Biscuit Periodicals, it gives me great pleasure to congratulate you on winning the custard cream competition. She held out a gold envelope. As I took hold of it, the photographer snapped a few pictures.

"Thank you very much." I lifted the flap, and took out the voucher which was for one hundred pounds.

"Thank you for coming down here today, Jill. I hope you enjoy your prize."

"I'm sure I will. Just one thing?"

"Yes?"

"How will I get the others? Will you post them to me?"

She looked a little puzzled. "Post what to you?"

"The other vouchers."

"What other vouchers?"

"For the other eleven months."

"I'm not sure I follow?"

"Isn't the prize meant to be one year's supply of custard creams?"

"Yes. One year's supply. That's what this voucher covers. We figured that two packets per week would be more than enough for anyone."

Two packets a week? Was she kidding? I could eat that many in a day!

"Oh? Right, of course. Thank you very much."

I took the tube back to the railway station. I'd already spent more on train tickets and taxi fares than the voucher was worth.

Two packets a week? Cheapskates!

ALSO BY ADELE ABBOTT

The Witch P.I. Mysteries:

Witch Is When... (Books #1 to #12)
Witch Is When It All Began
Witch Is When Life Got Complicated
Witch Is When Everything Went Crazy
Witch Is When Things Fell Apart
Witch Is When The Bubble Burst
Witch Is When The Penny Dropped
Witch Is When The Floodgates Opened
Witch Is When The Hammer Fell
Witch Is When My Heart Broke
Witch Is When I Said Goodbye
Witch Is When Stuff Got Serious
Witch Is When All Was Revealed

Witch Is Why... (Books #13 to #24)
Witch Is Why Time Stood Still
Witch is Why The Laughter Stopped
Witch is Why Another Door Opened
Witch is Why Two Became One
Witch is Why The Moon Disappeared
Witch is Why The Wolf Howled
Witch is Why The Music Stopped
Witch is Why A Pin Dropped
Witch is Why The Owl Returned
Witch is Why The Search Began
Witch is Why Promises Were Broken
Witch is Why It Was Over

The Susan Hall Mysteries:
Whoops! Our New Flatmate Is A Human.
Whoops! All The Money Went Missing.
Whoops! There's A Canary In My Coffee
See web site for availability.

AUTHOR'S WEB SITE
http:www.AdeleAbbott.com

FACEBOOK
http://www.facebook.com/AdeleAbbottAuthor

MAILING LIST
(new release notifications only)
http:/AdeleAbbott.com/adele/new-releases/

32678096R00130

Printed in Great Britain
by Amazon